The Mendings of
Merelda Manypockets

by Jodi Ember Roney

illustrations by Natalia Zanfardino

ISBN-13: 978-0692602010 (Lemon Lily)
ISBN-10: 0692602011

Printed in U.S.A

Dedicated to Joel, Mike, Nita, Logan and Bryce

CHAPTER 1

Merelda Gets a Message

Father Sun shone through the thinnest petal of Merelda
Manypockets' tulip-home, saying, *"Wake, Daughter, wake."* Merelda
felt the warmth spreading across her face, blinked up at the Sun, and
smiled. She pulled off her lilac-petal quilt and climbed sleepily up the
tiny spiral staircase that led to the top of the pistil-pedestal at the
center of her home. Then she spread her arms out wide and took in
the Sun's blessing till she overflowed with it.

After, Merelda gave her thanks and curtsied. She tidied herself, and finished by brushing her long golden-red hair and pushing her magic goggles to the top of her head to serve as a headband. Then she slipped her many-pocketed apron on over her yellow dress, secured a few belongings into a pocket here and there, and flew out through the top of her tulip-home to do her morning chores. The plants pulled themselves a little taller at her greeting, and when she was done whispering *"grow, grow"* to each in turn, Merelda flew to where the new crystals had been buried the night before by Tater and Tot, the garden gnomes.

She placed her hand over one of the energy lines, expecting to feel the gentle buzz of energy flowing to and fro between the crystals. But she gasped when a pins-and-needles sensation travelled up her arm instead. Frowning, she concentrated, and traced the trouble-signal back to its source: a Eucalyptus grove several miles away, past the big hill and beyond the lake.

Merelda was just making up her mind to go there after breakfast when up flew a very small brown bird with unusual yellow feathers atop his head. Those yellow feathers looked particularly sticking-out this morning, Merelda noted.

"Good morning, Reggie Wren. Would you like to join me for breakfast?"

Reggie shook his head and hovered mid-air, looking irritated. "No! No time to eat! Hurry Merelda, there's trouble in the Eucalyptus grove.

2

Will you come?"

"Of course, at once. But what is the trouble?" asked Merelda as she tightened her apron for the long flight and made sure her dozens of pockets were all securely shut.

"It's a tree. He's about to fall." And with that, Reggie Wren turned and flew away. Merelda was confused. Trees fell all the time; why was she needed?

She gave her head a little shake to free it from such questions and took to the air, flying fast up the hill. As she did, she gradually became larger and larger till she was the size of a barn owl. Merelda changed size as naturally as breathing, and typically with just as little notice. She was always the right size for the task, although she tended to grow no larger than owl-size without extra effort.

It wasn't till Merelda spotted a squirrel nibbling on an acorn on the far side of the hill that she remembered she had not yet had *her* breakfast. She patted around the outside of her pockets as she flew on, searching for a promising shape. And she was in luck. Merelda hadn't planted all the sunflower seeds yet, and there were still many resting in her turquoise and yellow striped pocket.

She removed a handful, careful not to drop any now that she was almost over the lake, and whispered

3

a question to the seeds. From deep within the seeds there came a happy 'yes' feeling, so Merelda began to eat as she flew over the water and out in search of the falling tree. Merelda didn't know it, but this would be her only meal until after sunset.

The Children See Merelda Flying

Farmer Tom was driving his children Lila Ticklegums and Billie B to their elementary school. They were each strapped in their car seats, and although the seats were comfy enough for sleeping and it was early in the morning, the children were awake. Lila had wavy brown hair and her head was tossed back confidently this morning. Billie's shoulders were slouched. He wasn't sure he liked school, but he kept his thoughts to himself most of the time. This wasn't one of those times.

"I see a boy running outside my window, keeping up with the car and jumping over each thing he sees." said Billie.

"For real, or in your mind's eye?" asked Lila, craning her neck to look out the window over her brother's shaggy blonde head, and seeing only the lake in the distance.

"In my mind," Billie said quietly. But Lila nodded and didn't tease him. She was good that way. Sometimes Billie thought she was as far from good as you can get, but not typically about things like this. After a minute she said, "And I see a giant walking along. He's so big that he doesn't have to run to keep up with the car. He's picking some trees now to use as decorations for his table... Do you think he owns

a vase big enough for those pines?"

Billie grinned at the image. "When he's thirsty, I bet he'll drink up the whole lake in one gulp!" Lila giggled, and Billie began picturing his running boy jumping over her giant's big toe in a splendid leap. Then Lila gasped, and pointed.

"Look, there! Flying over the lake! It's Merelda Manypockets. Not in my mind, for real!" exclaimed Lila. Billie looked, and sure enough, he could see a fairy with golden-red hair and a colorful apron streaking along over the water. She was flying very fast, and she looked like she was putting something into her mouth.

"Where do you think she's going?" asked Billie.

Lila shrugged. "We'll have to ask her when we get home later today." They were both quiet for a while as their father took a turn that led away from the lake. Then Lila made a promise. "I'll draw a picture of Merelda flying during art today. That way I won't forget to ask her where she was going." Billie said he'd do the same, and they began calling out the different colors they would need to draw all the pockets on her apron. They had an argument about whether or not red was required; Billie insisted that Merelda had a red pocket on her apron near the top and Lila said he was as wrong as wrong can be and that since she was the oldest she should know. But when Billie pointed out that red would be needed no matter what to draw Merelda's hair, she backed down.

Farmer Tom smiled as he drove. He liked to listen to his children, but seldom interrupted their conversations. He knew they had been talking about the Garden Fairy they said lived on their land, this Merelda with her many pockets and magic goggles with dial settings all along the sides of them. He had never been able to get the kids to explain to him what those dials were for, and he had a habit of wondering about that every time the kids mentioned Merelda.

Farmer Tom had never seen the fairy, but his children told him that she sometimes rode on the side of his hat while he was caring for the plants, and that this was why his hat was occasionally lop-sided. Farmer Tom liked picturing her up there. It was true that sometimes he got strange ideas about what to put on a particular plant, ideas like pouring a bit of root beer on the beets, and adding extra compost to the spinach patch on days when they looked just fine to his eyes. The notion that there was a tiny fairy giving him guidance made him feel warm inside, and he made good use of this when bad feelings threatened to overtake him. He spent a great deal of time in the garden, and made a point to wear his hat even on days when it was overcast. Even if Merelda was pretend, Farmer Tom liked that his children had such vivid imaginations, and that their fairy-friend cared about green growing things.

As he drove on, he found himself searching the skies, hoping to catch a glimpse of this Merelda Manypockets and wondering about the dials on the sides of her goggles. He was so intent about it that he almost missed his turn for the school.

Why Tree Can't Fall Yet

Merelda circled down lower as the Eucalyptus grove came
in sight. A rabbit with white and brown fur that she did not know
jumped up and down to get her attention and pointed excitedly
toward a path. Merelda flew low along the trail littered with long
strips of bark and leaves in various stages of decay, and had to swerve
to avoid a large mushroom family that had sprung up overnight. Soon
she came across several small squirrels chattering to one another, and
they pointed her onward as well. When the path finally opened to a
small clearing, Merelda saw at once what the problem was.

A very old Eucalyptus tree was on one edge of the clearing.
Merelda didn't need to put on her special goggles to see that he
was on the verge of falling. Right in the center of the clearing, in the
direction the tree would take on his way down, was Cowboy Roy

and his horse. The horse was tied to a large bush, and Cowboy Roy was lying propped up against a log with his hat pulled down over his eyes. His broad chest rose and fell in the smooth rhythms of someone deeply asleep. Merelda flew to the old tree and hovered near its trunk. She pulled out her wooden wand from its special pocket; the wand was crooked, but the magic that came from it was as straight as can be. Merelda used the wand to send the tree a blast of blessing-energy, but it flowed through him and immediately out his withered roots. The tree turned slightly toward her, and she could barely hear the wheezing voice of the Tree Spirit from deep within the tree. *"The squirrels tried to lure him, but… my roots… I will fall."*

Merelda tapped her lips, thinking. "I'll do what I can to move them, but first… Hmmmmm…" Several moments passed, then Merelda nodded briskly and pointed her wand skyward. Her clear fairy voice rang out as she sang:

"Blow, wind, blow,
Blow hard against this tree.
Buy me some time,
Or unlucky they will be!"

Brother Wind heard, and blew. Where the air had been still a moment before, now great gusts billowed through the clearing. Merelda had to flit off to the side quickly, lest she become pinned by the wind against the side of the aged tree.

There was a great sigh as the tree let himself relax into the wind's arms. The tree tilted visibly several feet toward the clearing, but Brother Wind held him firmly so he went no farther. The horse jumped at the movement and tried to get out of the way, but the rope around his neck held him firmly in place. He whinnied nervously, his brown mane whipping around in the gust of wind, and pawed the ground. Cowboy Roy's hat took flight and became ensnared in the leafy canopy of the tree, but Cowboy Roy himself slept on, oblivious.

"*Hurry, Merelda. I have business elsewhere,*" breathed Brother Wind.

Merelda then had an idea, and it felt right, so she acted. She shot upward till the land was well below her, with the lake glittering blue in one direction and the green treetops scattered thickly in another. But Merelda looked up toward the sky instead, casting about for Father Sun. He was there, behind a cloud. She raised her crooked wand and called out:

"*Father Sun,*
Shine down for me.
Reveal where your Great Stag
Is about to be."

From behind the cloud a beam of light shone down. Merelda went and hopped on it, swooshing down much as a child might on a very steep slide.

She went so fast that her pocketed apron and skirt billowed out. She couldn't see where she was going, and her bottom became quite hot. Finally she landed right on the top of the Great Stag's head with a thump. A puff of dander filled the air, and Merelda threw out her hand quickly to grab an antler so she wouldn't fall off.

"What's this?" growled Stag, and he gave his head a rough shake.

"Stop that!" cried Merelda. "I'm already dizzy. Give me a moment." She stood unsteadily atop the thick brown fur, took a deep breath, and abruptly sneezed. What a day she was having!

Stag Earns His Points

"Have you ever been chased by a man on a horse?" Merelda asked. She was now standing on a nearby rock, smoothing her skirt and trying discreetly to cool off her bottom.

"As many times as there are points on my antlers," said Stag in a bored tone, but his brown eyes twinkled at the question. He gave his head another shake that made Merelda cringe, and began nibbling the flat, scale-like leaves off an incense cedar tree.

Merelda knew a thing or two about full-grown bucks. The more points they had on their antlers, the more prideful they tended to be. She counted his points aloud, marveling, "....ten, eleven, twelve! I've never seen so many points on a deer before. You must be quite clever to have gotten away from men so many times."

Stag snorted, but didn't stop eating. Merelda liked the peppery smell the leaves and twigs gave off as he crushed them in his mouth. If the circumstances were different, she could have relaxed and made a day of enjoying watching Stag dine. But Merelda was on a mission.

"There are certain places where it is best not to be seen by a man, though, isn't that right?" Merelda called out the question in a loud voice. Stag turned his head to look at her, curious. Merelda lowered her voice to a hushed tone and kept talking. To hear her, Stag had to take a few steps closer.

"For instance, if a man caught sight of you in the Eucalyptus grove and had a horse he could ride, he'd catch you for sure. He'd take those beautiful antlers of yours as a trophy. There is no safe way to get out of the grove if there is a man and a horse around." As Merelda spoke, she made note that Stag's eyes were growing defiant.

"That's just not true!" Stag exclaimed. "Why, I could easily get away from a man-horse there. I'd make for the stream and run up it, then jump over the big rocks on the left bank and lose them in the pine trees that grow near the lake." He gave his head another shake as he lifted it high and said with certainty, "My antlers would grow by two points from such an adventure."

Merelda swiftly pulled her goggles down off the top of her head and took a peek at Stag's antlers. Across the crown of each white fork, the left and the right, she could see energy swirling where the points were just ready to push out. Stag was right; the potential was there.

"You're in luck!" Merelda cried excitedly. "You can earn two more points today! A man-horse is in the clearing in the center of the Eucalyptus grove right now, but you will have to hurry to reach them in time." Merelda still had her goggles on, and she gasped at what she now saw. As Stag registered her words, he quivered with excitement, and a golden energy began to swirl all around him.

"I'll go this very instant," Stag proclaimed, and turned to set off in the right direction.

"Wait!" Merelda instinctively cried out. As Stag turned back,

Merelda felt the words queue up that she was to deliver. She smiled, and felt Father Sun's warmth blossom within her, too.

> "You are to know that I asked Father Sun to take me to his Great Stag, and I was delivered to you. In letting this man-horse chase you, their lives will be saved. It is not for you alone that you go forth today."

When Stag heard her message, the swirling energy took on a steady form that settled over his body till the whole of him glowed brightly golden. His eyes blazed with a different kind of pride as he nodded to her.

"Would you like to ride upon my back to the grove?" he asked. Merelda blushed and curtsied, pushed her goggles back up to the top of her head, then flitted over to his broad back. Trying not to kick up too much dander, she took a handful of brown fur in each hand and called out that she was ready.

With a great leap, they were off. Merelda blinked and looked around. Even without the special lenses, the whole scene appeared to be glowing with light now. She looked up, and found Father Sun gazing down on them, a broad smile upon his face. Merelda smiled back.

The Ground Grows Rocks

When Merelda and Stag arrived at the Eucalyptus grove, they found a small crowd of forest creatures gathered at the edge of the clearing. Rabbits, squirrels, chipmunks, mice, skunks, frogs, and one pygmy marmot all craned their necks to see, while birds twittered from the branches of the trees. The birds reported their arrival first. "She's back, riding on a Stag!" The crowd murmured in response, then grew quiet.

Stag stopped where the path opened into the clearing, and Merelda flew into the air to take in the scene. Cowboy Roy and his horse were where they had been when she left, with Roy asleep and the horse still tugging futilely against his bindings. But the angle of the tree as it leaned over the man and horse was even more alarming than it had been, and all the life had gone out of the tree.

The hairs stood up on the back of Merelda's neck as she took this in. "I'm back," she announced to Brother Wind, and she suddenly felt quite insecure. What was she supposed to do now?

"Merelda, I had to send some wind elsewhere, and I must send the rest away soon. Hurry and do what you are here to do." The urgency was strong in Brother Wind's voice.

Merelda blinked. She pulled out her crooked wand and flew

over to where Cowboy Roy slept in the center of the clearing propped against a log on a patch of soft green grass. The winds were strongest here and she had to struggle to keep the wand from being pulled out of her hand. She landed on Roy's chest, which she hadn't planned on doing, but it was impossible to just hover here. She took a quick look at Stag illuminated by the glowing sunset, then steadied herself with a deep breath.

Her clothes and hair whipping around her, she poked Roy hard on the chest with her wand. "Wake, wake, Cowboy Roy!" she shouted, to no avail. She poked him again, this time giving him a blast of energy from the tip of her wand, but he merely used the energy to snore louder.

"Are you under an enchantment?" Merelda wondered aloud. She moved backwards and braced herself firmly by wedging one foot under his belt buckle. Then she stowed her wand safely away and pulled down her goggles instead. But there was no energetic explanation for why Cowboy Roy didn't wake. Through the goggles he merely looked like a healthy man that was deeply asleep. "This won't do," complained Merelda as she stowed her goggles back again on the top of her head.

Merelda flew a short distance to the side so she was no longer in the center of

the wind's gust, and tapped on her lips with her long fingers. "I could call on Sister Rain, but she can be so moody, and I don't feel like getting drenched..." Merelda blushed a bit as she watched her own thinking, wondering if she was being selfish. But no, Sister Rain didn't feel like the right person to call on. That left...

"I've got it!" Merelda exclaimed. Once more she pulled out her wand, but this time she pointed it, and all her attention, downward.

"Mother Earth, to him do prove
That soft can grow most hard.
Beneath his back sharp rocks do stack
So he'll up and leave this yard!"

Mother Earth heard, and answered. The soft green grass beneath Cowboy Roy abruptly withered. A rumbling sound came as several grey-streaked rocks began poking out between clumps of dead grass. One very large, pointy-looking rock pushed out of the ground so swiftly into the small of Cowboy Roy's back that it actually lifted him off the ground! His head tilted one way, and his brown boots the other, farther and farther, till Roy snorted suddenly and let out a gasp of pain. His eyes grew wide with alarm as he tried to sit up and found the best he could do was tumble off to one side.

"Well I'll be!" Cowboy Roy exclaimed loudly. He was on all fours, gazing at the pile of rocks as he shook his head to clear it from sleep, and wondering why he had chosen to sleep here of all places. He pushed up so that he was on his knees, felt the wind for the first time, and reflexively reached up to secure his missing hat to his head. But his hand froze mid-gesture as his eyes took in the sight of Stag silhouetted against the setting sun a mere twenty feet away.

"Well I'll be…" Cowboy Roy said again, this time in the softest of whispers. He rose quietly to his feet, all else forgotten. The wind pushed on him ferociously, but he seemed unable to notice anything but the presence of Stag. Without taking his eyes off the majestic deer, he untied his nervous horse, and quicker than a heartbeat he was mounted and turning the horse toward the stag.

Stag gave a confident shake of his head, and Father Sun in that instant filled the sky behind his antlers with royal shades of purple and red. Looking closely, Merelda could see where two new large points *had* knobbed out on the top of Stag's beautiful white antlers. Then the deer turned and raced up the path. Cowboy Roy let out a joyous whoop, and the chase was on.

Moments later, a tremendous crash shook the grove as Brother Wind softened his grip and the tree lay down at last. As the sound-reverberations faded, the air became filled by a dense silence. Dust and energy swirled around Merelda, the trees, and the gathered forest creatures.

Merelda sank to her knees, closed her eyes, and gave out her thanks in all directions. She felt the last touches of Father Sun as he filled the grove with his warmth, the whispers of Brother Wind as what remained of him circulated through the leaves, and the steady feel of Mother Earth beneath supporting them all.

As Merelda thought on her day's adventure, the words she had delivered to the Great Stag swam up in her mind, and she whispered them:

"It is not for you alone that you go forth today."

Tears appeared in Merelda's eyes as she realized the words were for her, as well. Then she saw through closed eyes Sister Rain before her, tracing her fingers down the fairy's soft cheeks. Merelda spread her arms out wide and took it all in as best she could. It was enough, gloriously enough, for one day.

The Purple Pocket

A long while passed. When Merelda opened her eyes again, it was dark. The forest animals blinked their eyes back at her, then quietly went about their business readying for the night. The familiar sounds of the evening crept back into the grove, and Merelda knew it was time to hang her purple pocket. But before she could do that, she had one last task to complete.

Merelda put on her special goggles and looked around for the groves' buried crystals. She knew they had to be nearby, and sure enough, when she looked for them through the enchanted lenses she was able to see a black tourmaline and a rose quartz crystal buried just ten feet from where she was kneeling. Merelda walked over, hovered her hands over the energy current that travelled between the two crystals, and opened herself to receive whatever messages were on hold for her there. She felt several squirmy and rather stale but distinctly gnome-flavored things travel up her arm and 'pop' in her head.

"Merelda, where are you?" began the message from Tater and Tot, the garden gnomes. It had been left several hours earlier. "The children hung drawings of you flying over the lake, and there's a buzz on the line about trouble in the Eucalyptus grove, and something about a fairy riding a donkey and a man that won't wake? We've looked everywhere for your purple pocket, so we know you aren't here. Where are you? Should we expect you for dinner?"

Merelda smiled. She liked that Tater and Tot missed her and had invited her for dinner. She patted around her apron to find where

22

her carry-crystal was hidden, and retrieved it from her red corduroy pocket along with a tiny broom fashioned from a twig and silky pieces of corn thread. Then she got to work.

Receiving messages was easy, but sending them took a bit of practice, and frankly, she didn't enjoy the process one bit. Merelda made little thought-bubbles in her mouth that contained what she wanted to say, then tried to blow them into a small hole the gnomes had drilled into her carry-crystal. Most popped prematurely, and she kept cleaning the sides of the crystal before she tried again even though no spit got on them. It took far longer than she wanted to load her crystal, and it reinforced her opinion that this whole business was a gnome thing and shouldn't be practiced by fairies. But once they were in, she carefully lowered the crystal into the energy line and frowned as her two thought-bubbles took the shape of little tadpole-like creatures and began to swim swiftly away into the energy current.

"You're to find Tater or Tot at my garden," she called after them, but she wasn't sure if they heard her or not. Once they had tails, thought-messages were such eager little things! If all went well, when either of the gnomes put their hands over their local crystals they would receive her message that all was good here, and her promise to fill their ears with stories upon her return tomorrow.

Then Merelda carefully used her tiny broom to brush away the stale trouble-signal from the crystals, and again used her carry-crystal to insert a general thought-message of reverence for the fallen tree and Stag (donkey, indeed!). When she was done, she put away her communication tools, blinked, and looked around.

She still had the goggles on, which was good, as there was a particular energetic she needed to find now in order to get to bed. Each living thing has energy lines connecting them, so the grove, like most places, was crisscrossed everywhere with energy lines. Merelda was now looking for a particularly strong, stable one. Two beings that deeply loved one another and didn't move around much would do quite nicely. In Merelda's garden, carrots and peas had this relationship, as did tomatoes and parsley. But Merelda wasn't in her garden, so she needed to broaden her search.

"Hmmmm…" she mused to herself. There was a pretty strong connection between a very pregnant white mushroom and a nearby sagebrush. Merelda sighed to herself. She was really much more tired than was her custom. She walked over to the energy line, careful not to bump the mushroom, and tugged on it with her hands. "This will do for tonight," she murmured to herself.

Merelda felt into her brown pocket and pulled out two enchanted but quite ordinary-looking clothespins, which she clipped to the top of her apron so they would be within easy reach when she needed them. Then she turned her attention to her purple pocket. It was at the bottom of her apron, near the center, and it had a special border made of her golden-red fairy hair. This was one of Merelda's most magical pockets, for within it lived her tulip home. She placed one hand on the tip-top of each end of the purple taffeta pocket, began to tug, and sang her homecoming song:

"Be full, pocket, be full,
For upon you I do pull.
It's time for me to rest
So no longer be compressed."

As Merelda pulled upon the purple fabric it lengthened, and soon her hands were stretched as high above her head as they could go. She gave the fabric a little shake and it detached from the bottom of her apron. With a swift, practiced movement, Merelda held the fabric up with one hand and used the clothespin to secure the fabric upon the line. "Almost there…" Merelda murmured as she clipped the second side of the fabric. Once it was secure, she shrunk a bit then stepped back to admire her work.

Where there had once been a gap between the sleeping white mushroom and the leafy olive-green sagebrush, there was now hanging in midair a large swatch of purple taffeta fabric with her golden-red hair woven along all the sides. Merelda pushed her goggles back up on her head, swept the fabric aside and stepped through.

Before her was home. A patch of enchanted ever-bloom tulips in shades of red, yellow and purple filled the air with a sweet clean scent. Beyond the tulips, as far as the eye could see, there stretched an old-growth redwood forest shimmering with magic in the moonlight.

Ferns, ivies and wildflowers peeked through the undergrowth that bordered her tulips to the rear, and several crickets were nestled there singing their nightly song. Under the sound of their music, you could hear the gentle rhythmic crash of the ocean's waves gracing a beach off to the left and downwards, well out of sight. To the immediate left of her tulip patch, a series of boulders let a creek babble down them, and in a small pond at the base of the last boulder was a pool where three goldfish lived. To the right of her tulip patch, a group of magically enhanced huckleberry bushes grew. They were always covered in big ripe berries. Convenient, since Merelda loved huckleberries.

Merelda let the purple pocket-curtain fall closed behind her and sighed in relief to be home at last. She grew smaller and smaller,

and she was just realizing how hungry she was when she noticed a bowl had been placed beneath her biggest yellow tulip, the one she slept in most often. As she approached, she found that the bowl contained a honeycomb dripping with fresh honey and a mound of newly picked huckleberries.

There was a note pinned down by the bowl:

we heard of your adventures and thought you might forget to eat. Love, the bees and the berries

"That's so sweet, thank you!" Merelda said as she sank down to the moss-covered ground and began eating her meal. Before her hands got too sticky she remembered to pull a white cloth napkin out of her yellow-satin pocket. When she was finished, she put the bowl into the little pond to soak overnight. The goldfish gurgled their thanks as they began nipping at the bits of honey and berry still left in the bowl. Merelda dipped the cloth in the water, gave it a small scrub, wrung it out and laid it to dry atop one of the smooth boulders.

Stifling one last yawn, Merelda flew in through the top of her yellow tulip-home. She pulled the lilac-petal quilt on her bed up to her chin and whispered a simple prayer. Quicker than you could say "bishop," she was fast asleep.

CHAPTER 2

Myrtle Magpie's Nest

When Merelda pulled back the hanging fabric of her purple pocket early the next day, she had a blessing ready for the mushroom babies she was sure had sprouted up. Instead, what she saw made her gasp and pull back. She shook her head, confused, and slowly poked her head out again for a longer look. She was no longer on the forest floor, and she was looking at, of all things… herself!

Her reflection was appearing inside a simple hand-mirror in a thin green wooden frame. The mirror was nestled into a wall made of sticks and mud. There were also feathers and purple pebbles placed here and there, and other objects that invited further exploration. Merelda stepped fully out from behind her pocket and looked around, blinking. There

wasn't just one wall; Merelda was in a large, dome-shaped nest.
It had a clay floor lined in moss and grass, and morning light streamed in through a rounded entrance on either side of the nest.

"Rose's thorns!" Merelda exclaimed. There was no doubt; she was in the home of Myrtle Magpie. Myrtle herself was nowhere to be seen.

Merelda felt a rush of protectiveness as she turned to regard her purple fabric. Its uppermost corners were tucked sloppily into a sloped place where the walls of the nest ended and the ceiling dome began. Her magic clothespins were nowhere to be seen, but luckily her fairy-hair border was still perfectly intact. "Myrtle can't have you, no matter how much she loves the color purple!" She gave the fabric a protective pat to reassure it, then pursed her lips and performed the special magic that turned her purple fabric back into a pocket on her apron.

As she did, her thoughts drifted. Merelda had emerged from her tulip-realm and found herself in strange places before. Once she had discovered her purple pocket plastered to the side of Farmer Tom's black rain boot—what a ride that had been! And just last summer Merelda had found her entryway barred by the chest of a sleeping gnome. Yes, it *was* true that he was a traveling gnome and didn't know her personally, but you would think a gnome of all creatures would know better than to use fairy cloth as a blanket! Once she had poked him awake with her wand, she had given him a stern lecture on how to tell what belongs to a garden fairy. She would have to re-educate Myrtle on that point soon, too. She had a rather nasty daydream of giving Myrtle a few pokes with her wand, but she guiltily shook these from her head.

Now that her pocket was put away, Merelda could see more of the nest. Near her feet behind where the pocket had been hung was a large circular strip of leather covered with dozens of cream-and-brown beads and one large turquoise and silver broach. Merelda's eyes narrowed as she recalled having seen that broach on the front of Cowboy Roy's hat. This was his hatband! Myrtle must have had to work quite hard to free it from his hat and transport it here.

"If all you lost in that grove was your hatband, you should count yourself lucky, Cowboy Roy," Merelda said in a clipped tone. But just to make sure, Merelda pulled down her special goggles and carefully arranged them over her eyes. Objects that had been owned by a human usually took on an echo of that human's personality, so Merelda had learned over the years. One should never take into their home something man-made unless they first made sure it truly wanted to be there. In the case of the hatband, it appeared content and was giving off a faint pink sleepy energy. Merelda thought of how snugly Cowboy Roy had been sleeping in the clearing surrounded by all those trees, and the corners of her mouth lifted in a smile. "Welcome to your new home, sleepy head."

But as Merelda continued to wear the goggles, she got the feeling that something was not quite right in Myrtle's nest. Her own pocket didn't want to be here, but that echo of complaint was already fading. No, it was something else. Merelda began walking around the nest with her special lenses in place. The nest was large, about two feet across. The domed ceiling felt spaciously high enough to Merelda in her current tiny sleeping-size, but something in the nest was giving off the feeling of... what? Merelda sent out little energetic probing-feelers in all directions. Ah, there—Merelda could now clearly taste the charcoal-ash flavor—something felt trapped, and was angry about it.

"Hmmmm..." Merelda tapped her lips as she meandered around, surveying the things that had caught Myrtle's eye over the years. Here was a piece of tin foil, and there was a bit of sparkly red and gold ribbon, but neither had any personality. She found a Christmas ornament shaped like an owl and giggled despite her focus. Myrtle had been overheard squawking to the other birds that she already shared her nest with an owl and couldn't make room for another. Then Merelda's eyes settled on a small music box with a ballerina on the top, the kind you could wind to make the ballerina turn, and Merelda shivered. That used to belong to Neighbor Ella. It radiated a nervous energy that made the hairs on Merelda's arms stand up.

"Don't you worry. I won't make you go back to Ella's house," Merelda reassured the music box.

Merelda's curiosity carried her a bit further along, and her gaze came to rest on a shiny metal toy sheriff's badge near one entrance to the nest. The badge had a puffed-up appearance that was visible through the goggles. Merelda gazed at it for a long time before saying, "You have played sheriff with Billie B, and you know your right from your wrong. Are you enforcing the rules here?"

The badge seemed to swell even larger in response, then it opened its clasp, and its sharp stickpin fell out and protruded into the entryway. "Ouch," Merelda whispered, and made a mental note to leave by the hole on the opposite side of the nest.

It was then that Merelda spotted the real source of the disturbance. On the other side of the entrance, ensnared in the sticks and clay, was a girl's barrette crafted in the shape of a dragonfly. It had been fashioned out of silver wire and purple beads, and the sides of the beads were faceted so that they sparkled in the morning light. One wing was bent, and through Merelda's goggles she could see that the barrette was giving off smoky-looking waves of red and black anger at being trapped here. The charcoal-ash taste was back and was so strong that Merelda wanted to spit, but did not.

Merelda fluttered her fairy wings, and moments latter she was standing next to the barrette. "Lila Ticklegums made you at school, and you used to go flying with her, didn't you?" The red dissipated a bit, and green pulses came from the barrette as if to say 'yes.' Lila had been awarded honorable mention at her elementary craft contest for having created the barrette, and although Lila still had the certificate taped to her wall, the barrette itself had gone missing a few weeks back. Merelda remembered Lila, eyes puffy from crying, asking everyone if they had seen her dragonfly and saying she couldn't fly without it.

"Would you like me to take you back to Lila?" Merelda asked, and swallowed a few times to clear the bad anger-taste out of her mouth. Green and gold bands of energy puffed out along the wings, and Merelda had her answer. "Okay, I'll see what I can do."

She briefly flirted with the idea of taking the barrette now and leaving, but that didn't feel right. No, the solution would present itself at the right moment, and it was going to involve Myrtle. Sighing, Merelda walked over to the center of the nest. As she did, she adjusted herself so that she would be just a wee bit larger than the magpie. She safely stowed her goggles back up amidst her hair and settled herself down on some moss to wait for Myrtle's return.

The Fairy Gift

It wasn't long before a thumping sound announced Myrtle's arrival as she landed in the entryway guarded by the sheriff's badge. "It's a good day, good day," Myrtle called out, then without missing a beat began making a harsh, chattering song of *wock-a-wock*. But her song came to an abrupt stop as she hopped into the sheriff's pin and let out a shrill cry of pain.

"Curses you!" she screeched and angrily swung closed the pin, holding it in place with one black claw and using her bright yellow beak to shut the clasp. "Stop opening or I peck you!"

Merelda noted the half-dozen inflamed patches on Myrtle's otherwise white belly. Myrtle had shiny black feathers and her wings were mostly black, but there was one large white patch high on each wing and she had a streak of yellow surrounding each eye. Myrtle had an extra long tail, even for a magpie, and it shined a lovely iridescent blue-green color in the morning light. But the look in Myrtle's eyes right now was not lovely.

Myrtle hopped over to her mirror to look at her belly. "Poor tummy! What I ever do to you, bad badge?"

"You're holding the dragonfly barrette against her will," Merelda said. Myrtle jumped so high she almost hit her head against the ceiling.

"*Wock!* What you doing here? My home!" Myrtle screeched, then began looking about frantically for the purple fabric. "Where you put it? My purple! Myrtle loves purple! I found it! Not yours, mine!"

Merelda breathed deeply so the color wouldn't rise in her face and slowly stood up. As she did she grew a few more inches in size, but she made herself stop when she felt the nest sag under her weight. In a firm voice she said, "Myrtle, you know quite well that the purple fabric you took marks the entryway to my home and must always remain untouched."

Myrtle had the decency to look uncomfortable as she shifted her weight from one claw to the other. "But was not *in* garden. Was far from garden. Was different shade of purple, not yours, and, *wock,* no fairy hair..." Myrtle looked around hopefully, wanting to show Merelda the fabric and have her claim be true.

"It is mine, Myrtle. It has my fairy hair hem, too. See, it's here now," and Merelda held up her apron so the small bottom-most purple taffeta pocket was stretched between her hands. Looking

closely, you could see the tiny golden-red border of fairy hair stitched all around the pocket. The border shimmered with fairy magic. "The same rules apply that always have; even though you like it, you can't have it, regardless of where you find it hanging."

"But it's purple," Myrtle said in a small voice, and looked away.

"Do you like Cowboy Roy's hatband?" Merelda asked.

"It's brown and blue. You take it, too?" Her voice sounded sulky and defiant at the same time.

"The hatband can stay. But it's not often you have a fairy over to set things right in your home, so listen." Her voice sounded angrier than she intended, so Merelda shrank in size a bit to compensate, and tried again with a gentler tone. "I ask that you trust me. How long has the sheriff's badge been stabbing you?"

"*Wock-a-wock*... A few weeks..." Myrtle ruffled her feathers uncomfortably, and began edging toward the exit, looking like she wanted to fly away. In seeming answer to her movement, the sheriff's badge let its clasp open again. The pin fell outwards with its tip protruding into the exit. "*Wock!*" Myrtle cried in sudden furry as she leaped backwards. "Why you pricking me?!?"

"He's trying to punish you for keeping the dragonfly barrette here when it doesn't want to stay. You know Lila has been looking for it, too." Merelda was careful to keep the judgment out of her voice, as the badge was doing enough judging for everyone. But it did pain her to remember Myrtle picking through the compost pile next to the farmhouse, in easy earshot of Lila as she asked if anyone had seen her barrette. Now that she thought about it, Merelda recalled how swiftly Myrtle had taken to the air after that, squawking that it was about to rain, though the sky had been a bright blue.

"It's purple... so pretty..." Again, Myrtle's voice had gone soft. She hopped over to admire the barrette, and a glazed look came over her eyes.

Here it is, Merelda thought. She had been waiting for the solution to present itself, and it just had. She walked over to the sheriff's badge. "Badge, will you promise to stop sticking Myrtle if she lets me take the dragonfly barrette home to Lila right now?"

The badge swelled importantly again at the thought of an

agreement. "I'll take that as a yes," Merelda said as she placed the pin securely in its clasp. Then she plucked one of her beautiful long golden-red hairs from her head and tied it securely around the badge's clasp. "That's fairy hair; it's binding," she said to both Myrtle and the badge. The hair wriggled and transformed into a sturdy-looking band that appeared to be made of solid gold. The badge sighed with pleasure at the contact.

Merelda turned to Myrtle. "Now I will give you a special fairy gift that will mark you as unique among all birds. But first you must let me have the barrette, and you must vow to not take it from Lila again, regardless of where she leaves it." Myrtle looked unsure for a moment, but her curiosity got the better of her.
"I promise," she said, and then, "A gift? A fairy gift?"

Merelda carefully took the barrette down from the wall of the nest and reshaped it till its wing straightened. It was big, so Merelda exhaled a smallness breath on it till it had shrunk to a size that would fit easily in her blue chenille pocket. Once she had tucked it away, she turned to face Myrtle, whose dark eyes had grown large as she watched the magic.

Merelda drew her wand, and Myrtle began flapping her wings and backing away, *wocking* loudly in fear.

"Myrtle, calm down. You'll like this, I promise. Just go over to the mirror so you can see it happen. Trust me, I'm a fairy."

Myrtle rocked in place for a minute, then hopped over to stand in front of the mirror, her eyes wide with excitement and fear. "What you do?"

Merelda pointed her wand at Myrtle's chest and called out:

"Feathers upon Myrtle's chest
Let all see the outcome of this test.
So long as Myrtle's promise is true
Purple you will be, through and through!"

So it came to pass that the feathers upon Myrtle's chest turned
a brilliant shade of purple. They turned, in fact, the exact shade as
Merelda's purple taffeta pocket. That is where Merelda left Myrtle,
wocking at herself in the mirror happily. Merelda patted the sheriff's
badge on her way out to feel its gratitude reverberate up her arm.
Then she took to the air, happy to be flying again. Just one more
errand and she could return to her garden.

Mushroom Light

It didn't take long for Merelda to find the clearing in the Eucalyptus grove. Sure enough, there *were* baby mushrooms all sprouted in a ring around where Merelda had hung her purple pocket the night before. In the center of the ring were her two ordinary-looking but actually quite magical clothespins.

Merelda allowed herself to become the perfect size for the fairy ring as she landed in its center. She picked up the clothespins, brushed them off, and returned them to their brown pocket on her apron. Then Merelda curtsied to all the assembled mushrooms and the nearby sage bush.

"Mother Mushroom, may I bless your babies?" The baby mushroom caps all nodded happily this way and that, while their mother's cap gave a much more dignified tilt toward her in response.

Merelda grinned. She loved mushrooms with good manners. She pulled out her crooked wand and sang aloud the blessing that had come to her earlier that morning:

"Bless your babies,
Small and white;

Long will shine
Their mushroom light!"

Merelda tapped each of the white mushroom babies gently on the tops of their heads. In response to her magic, their caps turned a bright red color sprinkled with white dots, marking them as having been blessed by a fairy. Each white dot shone like a flashlight. Merelda had to shield her eyes by the time she was finished. It was intense to stand inside a fairy ring of newly blessed babies!

Merelda posed a question to the young ones. "Would any of you like to come bring your light into my garden? My gnome friends, Tater and Tot, require mushroom-light to work by underground as they tend the roots of our plants."

Two of the babies began to rock this way and that with excitement. Merelda turned to their mother. "With your permission, of course, Mother Mushroom." Merelda said this out of politeness. She knew that mushrooms were wanderers, and that these babies would soon be out exploring this grove and beyond.

Mother Mushroom nodded in her careful way again, so Merelda continued. "Would you two like to come with me right now, or shall I come back for you in a few days?" Merelda quieted herself and listened closely with her fairy ears. She heard a faint *"now, now."* So Merelda plucked her two new mushroom friends, and she made sure to hold them firmly by the stalk, as mushrooms of all ages appreciate a firm hand.

Merelda briefly considered shrinking the mushrooms and putting them in a pocket, but decided against it. Their caps were really quite delicate. So she held one in each hand, and told them, "No wiggling while we're in the air, or I might drop you by accident. Are you ready to fly right this instant?"

"*Yes, yes!*" was the response. So Merelda took to the air, holding a not-too-wriggly red-capped glowing mushroom in each hand. She flew out of the grove, over the lake, and beyond the big hill toward her garden and Farmer Tom's home.

Billie B's Dream

Billie B sat quietly at the kitchen table, his fingers absentmindedly curling a chunk of blonde hair that grew on the very top of his head. There was a piece of paper in front of him and many crayons in easy reach, but for several minutes the page had remained blank. He was wishing very much that his mother hadn't died, and was missing her something terrible.

"Would you like to crack some eggs, Billie?" Farmer Tom asked. Milk and a box of pancake mix were already on the kitchen counter, as was a large wooden bowl and a whisk. Farmer Tom held an egg out, but Billie shook his head. He got up from the table though, and came to sit on the stool next to the counter. Billie watched silently as his father cracked eggs into the bowl and began searching in a drawer for a measuring cup. He noted that his father was getting some things in the drawer sticky with egg goo. His mother wouldn't have liked that one bit and might have brought out her big voice over it, especially if he had been doing it instead of his father. This made him miss her even more.

"What's on your mind?" asked Farmer Tom. His brown hair was pointing in several directions today, but his brown eyes were kind and they looked straight at Billie.

"I had a strange dream," Billie replied, gazing closely at the countertop. Sometimes he saw faces in the patterns of the wood grain, but not today.

"Well, let's hear it," Farmer Tom said as he poured milk into the batter and began to stir the contents of the bowl. A bit of it slopped out and landed on Farmer Tom's hairy toes.

"Mmm…" Billie was quiet for a while as his father got a towel and wiped off his foot. Billie traced his fingers through the flour-mix that had fallen on the countertop. His father resumed working on the pancakes, but Billie could feel that his attention was mostly on him. "I dreamed I was a skeleton, then after a while I became just the top part. You know, the skull." Billie glanced up as he felt a pulse of anxiety; he knew it was weird to dream he was a skull. But his father just kept stirring, so after a while Billie continued. "I stayed that way a long time, just lying outside somewhere. I could feel the seasons changing around me, but I was deep inside the skull and nothing could touch me."

"Then things changed, and I was a butterfly. I think I somehow pushed my way out of the skull. I stood on its top and my wings were stretched out, but I didn't fly. That's how the dream ended." Billie B looked down, suddenly feeling very self-conscious. He made his fingers lie still against the countertop.

There was a long silence, and Billie heard the bowl being placed on the counter. He felt his father's hand on his shoulder. "You know why that butterfly didn't fly, right?" Billie shook his head. He was sad all over.

"Because the butterfly's wings have to dry first. After he's born, a butterfly will sit and fan his wings for a while, then he'll fly away when the moment is right. That's natural."

Billie met his father's eyes. His shoulders relaxed, and he gave his body a quick shake.

Lila Ticklegums came running into the room. She had a long piece of rainbow-colored silk in one hand and a big red silk in the other, and because she was running they were streaming out behind her.

"Look, I'm flying again!" she called out, then skidded to a stop and tilted her head down till her nose was almost touching the countertop. "See? She's back!" Lila hollered into the wood.

Billie looked. Clipped neatly in Lila's wavy brown hair was her purple dragonfly barrette. He hadn't seen it for quite some time, and he recalled Lila accusing him of hiding it from her on purpose. It looked bigger than he remembered. "Where did you find her?" Billie asked.

"She was clipped to my drawing of Merelda flying over the lake. Come fly with me, Billie!"

Lila held out the rainbow silk to her brother, who took it in his hands as he slid off the stool. Billie looked up at his father, who winked and gave a little nod. Then Billie was off in a flash, the silk streaming behind him as he chased his sister down the hallway and out the front door of the house.

The grass felt damp beneath his bare feet, the sun was shining, and Billie felt a warm smile spread throughout his whole body as he and his sister flew out into Merelda's garden.

CHAPTER 3

Neighbor Ella's Spell

Merelda was lounging on a branch of an oak tree. After her afternoon chores were done, she had come up the tree to see how tightly the acorns were wearing their caps. She had found that on even the chattiest acorns, the caps were still fitting snuggly. Brother Wind was in a calm mood today. He was gently pushing on the branches, so Merelda had placed a willing leaf into a pie-shaped notch and was letting herself be rocked. She was just beginning to doze off when she heard someone approaching the tree.

It was Lila Ticklegums. Lila normally ran from place to place, but today she was walking slowly, her head down and her shoulders stooped. From Merelda's vantage, she could see that for the first time in over a week, Lila's dragonfly barrette was not nestled in her brown hair. Lila slumped down on a rock under the oak tree and looked as sad as sad can be.

"Lila?" Merelda called out the girl's name as she flew down

to join her. Adults could not see her, but Lila could still see Merelda and the gnomes that worked in the garden. "What's wrong?" Merelda asked as she landed on a nearby rock.

"I can't tell you," Lila moaned. But then a moment later she burst out, "Oh Merelda, it's terrible! I don't like my room anymore. I'm afraid to be in it." Tears oozed down Lila's face, and Merelda could see that these weren't the first. Lila must have been crying all morning. Her hair was hanging in lifeless hanks and had the clumpy look of someone who had tossed about all night and hadn't bothered with a comb.

"But you've always loved your room." Merelda had visited Lila's room in Farmer Tom's house many times over the years, and it was a joyous space. If Merelda had been a little girl instead of a fairy, perhaps

she would have had a room much like Lila's. Well, not so messy, but the love in it made Lila's room feel wonderful despite the disarray. "What happened?"

Lila sniffed and wiped at her eyes. "Yesterday Papa told me to take vegetables from our garden to Neighbor Ella. You know she can't grow anything. I hate going over there and I told him so, but he said it was the right thing to do. I couldn't find Billie so I went alone. Ella's got all these ballet trophies and things, and I knocked it and it broke and she got angry."

Lila looked at Merelda, her green eyes wide and the white rims streaked with red. "She was really scary. It was just an accident."

"You didn't mean for anything to get broken" Merelda said. Lila nodded and wiped her nose. A trail of snot streaked her hand, and Lila wiped it absent-mindedly on her jeans. Merelda cringed and resisted the urge to mumble a cleaning spell. When Lila spoke again, she sounded a bit more defiant.

"But Ella didn't care. She was all red. She grabbed me by my arm and it hurt, and she demanded that I tell her what my favorite thing in the world was. I wanted her to let go, and I thought if I told her, she would. I said my room." Lila's face seemed to collapse in on itself. "Now I don't want to be there," she choked out in a squeaky voice. Her tears started flowing again, and this time Lila put her hands up over her face.

"That must have been scary, to have an adult treat you that way. I would have been scared, too." Merelda took a deep breath, hoping Lila would take the hint and have one, too.

She didn't. But Lila did lower her hands as she took quick sips of air in a jerky way. "She was really, really mean."

"What happened next?" Merelda prompted.

"She told me to go home and look; that my room would be different now, and I would never be happy there again." More tears, and a look of fear came into Lila's face as it twisted with emotion. When she spoke again, panic that verged on hysteria colored each word. "And it's true! My room did look wrong. It felt wrong, too. And when I tried to go to sleep last night, I couldn't. It was extra dark and it seemed like the clock always showed the same time... I hate Neighbor Ella! I hate hate hate her!" Lila's body tensed as the anger peaked, but it was gone again as quickly as it had come. She was left looking limp and confused, and very sad. She kicked at the grass near her feet and wiped at her nose again.

So there it was. Merelda tapped her lips, wondering. She knew humans could cast spells without knowing they were doing so. It troubled her to think that Neighbor Ella had actually meant to cast this one. Words were powerful. If the listener agreed with them, they could become as binding as fairy hair.

Merelda needed to talk to Lila's Potent right now.

Lila was still looking down at the grass, so Merelda began. She made a complicated hand gesture in the air. Where her fingers traced, a golden light sparkled briefly and faded. She also spoke aloud in Potent language, which was pitched in a frequency that was probably too high for humans to understand. *"Stay and speak with me, please?"* If Lila heard anything, it was akin to the whistle of wind through leaves.

Merelda turned and spoke to Lila. "Thank you for sharing this with me, Lila. I will see what I can do." She paused for a moment, wondering how to get Lila to leave. "Could you gather some lemons for me? A dozen will do. Please wash them and leave them in a pile over by the pumpkin patch." The lemon tree and pumpkin patch were both on the other side of the house, well out of sight of this oak.

Whatever Lila had expected, it wasn't to be asked to work. The lemon tree had thorns on it, too! Looking like she was about to cry again, she nodded to Merelda. She slumped slowly away, making a point to drag her feet so she would get the most mud on her shoes.

Merelda pulled down her special goggles and spun a dial on the side of each eyepiece carefully forward till she head three clicks. She blinked as the scene before her adjusted, and then let out a sigh. Lila's Potent stood before her.

Lila Ticklegum's Potent

Despite her concern for Lila, Merelda felt joy bubble up in her heart as she regarded the lovely Spirit-being. Each Potent she had encountered had this affect on her. It had taken Merelda much tinkering and experimentation to be able to see them through her special goggles, and even longer to learn their language, but it had taken her no time at all to grasp that Potents were good.

As Merelda understood it, each Potent was an embodiment of one human's essence. They were here to work with their human as a guide. The Potents called themselves the 'Guardians of Individualized Potential,' but Merelda found the name cumbersome and called them "Potents" instead. Not for the first time, Merelda wondered if she was the only fairy who had ever seen or spoken with a Potent.

As was the way with Potents, Lila's Potent looked like an adult version of Lila. The eyes were the same as Lila's except that they looked even brighter, and the face that surrounded the eyes held great wisdom. She had a woman's body, but Merelda knew she was a Spirit-being, with Spirit-being powers. With Merelda's goggles in this special setting, Lila's Potent was in color, but everything around her appeared in varying shades of grey and no longer seemed real.

"Has her room changed?" Merelda asked. She had learned that Potents considered straightforwardness polite, so she obliged.

"Her room is the same. She is releasing and projecting her fear into the space, but none has become anchored in any items. I have cleared it all away." The Potent's voice was so lovely that Merelda closed her eyes to savor it. The sounds travelled through her, nourishing her much as

Father Sun's light did. Those two must be related, Merelda thought.

"*Does this warrant an intervention?*" Merelda hoped the answer would be yes. She had come to understand that there were strict rules the Potents had to follow when interacting with humans. Several years ago when Mother Mary had been near death, she had been able to see and talk with her Potent for a few days. This had been called an intervention. Mary had told her children and Farmer Tom about

her Potent, and when she died, she had gone with her Potent willingly. There had been a grace to it that Merelda had admired. Merelda thought briefly of the recently fallen tree and felt the reverence surrounding each memory merge within her.

In answer to Merelda's question about intervening, the Potent looked off into the distance and held her arms out straight before her. She swiftly grew taller and taller, and her hair began to swirl as the energy around her built. She touched her palms together, and then swung her arms out smoothly so they pointed directly out from her sides.

Merelda's whole body began to tingle and vibrate as she gazed at what was now before her. Where the Potent's left arm had traced, there hovered a vision in mid-air of Lila's room, shining with light. Where her right arm had traced, there was a mirror-image vision of Lila's room, but this scene was much darker. Lila sat on the bed in each parallel vision, and she was the age of a teenager. In the left scene, where all was bright, she looked healthy and her eyes were playful. She was leaning forward, and with a deft hand was applying a vibrant shade of orange nail polish to her toes. In the right scene, her shoulders were slumped, her cheeks had a puffy, sagging look, and her eyes were dull. She was gnawing on her fingernails. It made Merelda's stomach hurt like it did when she viewed a plant that was rotting from the inside.

Merelda hands flew up to her face and the motion changed her goggles dial settings. When she righted them again, the scene was gone, and the Potent was again adult-sized and her arms were down, with her fingers touching casually in front of her waist. She looked thoughtful.

"*What was that?*" Merelda asked. She was scared by what she had seen in the right-most vision, and her words quavered such that she wondered if she could be understood.

She was. "*Now is a pivotal time in Lila's life, as you just saw. Lila's room is a reflection of herself. If Lila continues to believe her room is a poisonous place, the belief will poison her perception of herself. If this perception is corrected, then she'll continue to thrive as she has been, loving herself without even knowing that she is doing so.*"

The Potent placed her hand on Merelda's shoulders. Merelda blinked, noticing that the Potent was now the same height as Merelda so their eyes gazed into one another. But Merelda didn't remember changing size—had the Potent grown smaller, or Merelda larger? "*Don't talk with Lila again today. She must not link the gift I am about to give her with you. But if you stay out of sight, you can come to her room tonight to bear witness.*" The Potent winked in a playful way, squeezed her shoulder, and then disappeared. Merelda was unnerved. She was used to being the one who changed size and made things disappear!

With a shaky hand, Merelda reached up and spun her goggles dial settings three more clicks in a backwards direction. The world returned to its normal color with all the energy lines spread out before her. Just as Merelda was about to take off the goggles, she noticed that there was a cricket she knew waiting patiently off to one side. She turned to greet him, although she didn't really want to talk to anyone right now.

"Hi, Cricket Nick. Were you waiting for me?" Merelda asked in a flat voice. She wondered why Nick was coming to see her by daylight, but didn't ask.

"Yes. I limped here. I seem to have lost my crick." Nick shook one of his legs.

Merelda looked at the cricket through her special goggles, and sure enough, where there were normally two tightly coiled springs in the cricket's strong hind legs, she instead saw a loose dangling coil in one of them. "Oh, your spring's sprung," Merelda sighed.

She patted around the outside of her pockets, trying to remember where she kept her magic corkscrew. "This would never work if I wasn't a fairy," Merelda mused to herself as she set to attaching the loose end of the dangling coil to the sharp tip of her magic corkscrew. As she turned it and the coil got tighter and tighter, she wondered about Lila and what it was like to be human, not knowing they are able to make things happen through the power of their belief. She shuddered again as she thought of how different the two teenage Lila images had been, and heard Cricket Nick give a sharp chirp.

"That's tight, Merelda," Cricket Nick warned. And so it was! Merelda hadn't been paying attention. With some difficulty, she looped the end in place and stepped back to watch Nick give a practice jump.

The jump carried him out of sight, but Merelda doubted the legs were of equal tightness now.

"That's the price you pay for free fairy work," she called out, meaning to be funny. But the words sounded bitter to her ears, and she was glad that Nick was out of earshot. She was really quite tired.

The Potent's Gift

Merelda decided to nap in Lila Ticklegum's room. When she got there, Merelda saw that yes, the room was as happy a place as it had ever been on any of her past visits. Sure, yesterday's clothes on the floor so near to the hamper were a bit annoyed, and the day-old cup of milk on the side table was downright grumpy as it curdled, but otherwise all the items in the room radiated with Lila's innocent happiness. The room smelled like fresh laundry despite the fact that there was not a bit in sight.

Merelda found a paper plate with a mass of feathers glued onto it sitting on a shelf. The glue was dry and it was already near the edge of the shelf, so it would offer a good bed and view of the room. Merelda transformed herself into her smallest sleeping size, stepped gingerly onto a soft-looking yellow feather, and curled up for her nap. Hadn't she already tried this once today? Her thoughts started to blur as she drifted off.

It was fully dark when Merelda awoke. The first sound she heard was a springy, bouncy sound, and she wondered if Cricket Nick had come to complain. But then the singing began. It was Lila, jumping up and down on her bed, tossing her head and singing "This Little Light of Mine, I'm Gonna Let It Shine!" at the top of her lungs.

Merelda pulled on her special goggles as quickly as she could and strained to make sense of it all. The room was glowing with more light than it ever had before, as though Father Sun himself was inside every object. The items were vibrating slightly, abuzz with life and love and happiness. It was a beautiful vision, and it seemed Lila was seeing it, too!

Merelda spun her goggle settings quickly three clicks and the Potent came into view. She was standing in the center of the room, facing Lila, and she had her own hands pressed over her eyes. She was extremely tall again and her hair snaked out in all directions like it had earlier that day; power seemed to be radiating off her. Ah, that's it! Merelda whistled softly as she realized what gift the Potent was giving Lila. She was causing Lila to see the room as the Potent saw it.

"This is so good!" Merelda squealed, unable to keep quiet. She spun her goggles dials back to their normal energy setting, then she began hopping up and down on the pile of feathers, too, and she sang along with Lila, "Let it shine, Let it shine, Let it shine!" Merelda was so happy she was fit to burst.

Something changed. A door opened, and a light switch clicked. Lila saw her father standing in the doorway, and she leaped off the bed into his surprised arms. "Papa, Papa, Papa—do you see? Everything is ALIVE, and it all LOVES ME!" She was quivering all over in his arms such that he struggled to keep his footing.

"Whoa, Little Tickle, start over—what's happened?" asked Farmer Tom. He put her down and kneeled to look into her eyes, but Lila began tearing around her room. "It was here!" she shouted, picking up a picture book. "And here!" This time she picked up a stuffed lion. "And here, and here, and here, and everywhere!" She ran around the room, gesturing at each item, then twirled around in the center. "And it was in the walls and the ceiling and the floor and the bed! It was all full of love, and it all loves me!"

She leaped on the bed again and resumed bouncing. "I am so so so so so happy, Papa! Did you see the room glowing for me?"

Farmer Tom stood again and rubbed his forehead, then walked over to the bed. "I can't say I did, Lila, but I am happy for you. From where I stand, well... it seemed to me you were jumping up and down on your bed in the dark."

"What? That's crazy! The room was full of light!" Lila giggled and fell down on her bed, squirming around like a puppy.

Now that Farmer Tom had said it, Merelda knew it to be true. The lights *had* been off and it had been dark, but not for Merelda with her special glasses, or for Lila who was seeing through the Potent's eyes. What a miracle! Merelda hoped Lila would remember this her whole life.

Farmer Tom sat on the edge of Lila's bed, and Lila promptly snuggled into his lap. "I'm so happy, Papa." Farmer Tom stroked her cheek with the back of his hand. "That's good, Tickle. Do you think you can sleep?"

"Never!" shouted Lila, and Farmer Tom smiled. "Well, just try to keep your voice down so you don't wake Billie, okay?"

Merelda turned her goggle's dial three times again, curious. She saw Lila's Potent and Farmer Tom's Potent, each standing on either side of their humans. Farmer Tom's Potent looked so much like Farmer Tom that Merelda felt tears of joy come into her eyes. And Mother Mary's Potent was there, too, standing with them and gazing down adoringly at her daughter and husband. The sight gave Merelda a strange, airy, dreamlike feeling. She spun her goggle settings back to normal again quickly lest she intrude, put them safely away on the top of her head, and silently slipped out the bedroom window.

Merelda was so taken by her good feelings that she reached her destination before she realized where she was going. She had flown to Neighbor Ella's house. She waited for the reason to reveal itself to her, and soon enough, it did. "Right," Merelda murmured, her tone much subdued. "I have work to do here, don't I?" She had her answer already, so Merelda found an open window and slipped inside Ella's house.

CHAPTER 4

Neighbor Ella

"Oh my," mused Merelda as she stepped out from behind the thick drapes that hung over the windows in Ella's living room. There was a fire in the fireplace and the lights were on, but the room still seemed very dark. Merelda didn't have to put on her goggles to know that despair radiated from these walls and objects. This is what Lila's room could have become, Merelda realized. Dirty dishes were stacked in the adjacent kitchen, and there was a china cabinet against one wall whose door had been left open. But despite these signs of life, the house felt strangely unoccupied. Merelda's eyes found Neighbor Ella sitting in a chair, and they narrowed.

Ella was a young woman that looked old. She had brown hair tied back severely in a bun, and her face was very pale. Her green eyes had a pinched look, and they were somehow pale, too. Merelda found herself wondering if this woman ever let sunshine touch her. She was wearing a fluffy blue bathrobe that was threadbare in patches near the wrists and elbows where Ella clearly had a habit of plucking. The bathrobe also bulged oddly, giving Ella a lopsided pear shape. Merelda took a few steps to the side and decided a water bottle tucked against Ella's left hip was causing the bulge. There was a cup of tea on the small table next to Ella's chair, but it was cold and full to the brim. Lila's basket of vegetables was on the ground near the front door; it also didn't look like it had been touched.

"You don't appreciate what we share with you," Merelda said. As expected, Ella didn't react. She could not hear or see Merelda.

Merelda turned to see what was holding Ella's attention. The fireplace beside the large window Merelda had come through had an oak mantle over it. The mantle supported a series of trophies, plaques, framed pictures of playbills and a large photo of an elegant woman in a ballet costume. The largest ballet trophy was on the ground in front of the fireplace, shattered. It was clear that Ella had let it lie exactly as it had fallen.

"The girl did her a favor by breaking the trophy." The musical voice made Merelda jump. She looked around quickly, but could not

find the source of the words. She hid herself behind the mass of drapes, preparing to leave, and then realized that the voice sounded… good. It was the only thing in this house that felt right. But still, as she stepped out from behind the curtain again, she drew her wand and said:

"Wherever you are, let yourself be seen.
As it is, this feels kind of mean."

The crooked wand spurted some gold sparks, but nothing happened, as it wasn't really a spell. Merelda blushed a bright crimson color. The long moments stretched and all was silent. Merelda wanted the voice to speak again. She closed her eyes, and saw a vision of the sun going behind a cloud. A voice like the sun…

Merelda suddenly felt foolish again, but for a different reason. Of course Merelda and Ella weren't alone! She put on her special goggles, adjusted the settings till she heard the three clicks, and looked around the room.

Ella's Potent was standing a few paces behind Ella. She was grinning at Merelda, and she had a mischievous twinkle in her eyes. Her long brown hair was also pulled up in a bun, but on her the look was elegant. She was wearing a shiny robe that flattered her slender figure. Merelda found herself blushing again, but this time in delight. She knew her mouth was hanging open, but she did not care. The difference between Ella and her Potent was more striking than she had ever seen with any of Farmer Tom's family. *"You look so healthy! You make me want to dance,"* Merelda said in the high-language.

Ella's Potent laughed, and the sound was liquid gold that lingered in the air as music. She took several steps and pirouetted elegantly, her arms outstretched and her hands relaxed.

Merelda giggled. She felt as though she had just eaten a whole bowlful of huckleberries. Watching the Potent satisfied something deep inside. *"How do you do that?"* she asked.

"By being me," the Potent answered. It was the right answer.

Merelda remembered again that 'Potent' was short for 'the Guardians of Individualized Potential.' *"So Ella could be like you, even now?"*

"Yes, but she doesn't let herself know this." The Potent looked patient rather than sad as she spoke.

"What happened to Ella? Surely she was happy once. How did she get like this?"

In answer, the Potent let her eyes look out to the horizon. She grew swiftly taller and taller as she raised her arms before her, her palms touching. Merelda cringed, afraid of what she might see.

Merelda at the Ballet

When the Potent began swinging her arms open, Merelda instinctively closed her eyes. She opened them again and let out a yelp. She was no longer in Ella's house! She was on a stage, and there were hundreds of people in front of her all standing and applauding. Merelda was exposed!

She snatched off her goggles and quickly became her smallest possible size, then turned to see where she could hide. Impossibly large man-made objects were scattered around her, including brightly wrapped presents, candy canes, and the largest Christmas tree she had ever seen. Merelda swiftly flew up into the tree, but she recoiled mid-air when she realized it was made of plastic. Why would anyone create a fake plastic tree? Her sudden anger startled her as much as the plastic around her, but she quickly did her best to drop it and looked for the least appalling place to hide. She chose a wooden Christmas ornament shaped like a sleigh, and it rocked a bit as she settled into it. "At least you were once alive," she muttered to the wood of the sleigh. She took several deep breaths, and then enlarged herself till she was just the right size to look out over the side of the sleigh.

Merelda's eyes grew wide as she took in the scene onstage. From the back to the front, the stage was filled with rows of children and young adults all wearing ballerina costumes and other colorful outfits. Standing in the crowd near the front were two of the most peculiar people-shaped things Merelda had ever seen. One was a man-sized version of the red and blue nutcracker that Farmer Tom put on display at Christmas time, and standing next to him was a strange creature that appeared to be a mix between a human and a rodent. Both the nutcracker and the rodent thing were holding swords!

A little boy ran onto the stage just below her. He was Billie B's age, but he was not any child Merelda had ever seen. The clothes he was wearing looked normal enough, but he had slippers on his feet that looked like Lila's special dancing shoes. He slowed down as he approached the lady standing in the very front and center closest to the audience. He bowed and held out a bouquet of white roses to her.

This lady was dressed all in white lace with an elaborate tutu that stood stiffly out from her hips. As the lady moved to take the flowers from the boy, Merelda saw that the lady in white was Ella! Her mouth dropped open in surprise.

Ella held the flowers up and curtsied to the audience. Something very big to the side of Merelda began moving, and she fearfully ducked her body down into the sleigh. It jiggled haphazardly mid-air from her movement. When it had stopped rocking enough for her to safely peek out, she saw that the thick burgundy drapes that had been gathered at either side of the stage were being drawn closed.

Their sounds were muffled now, but Merelda could still hear the audience clapping and whistling as the people on stage began moving toward the exits. The strange rodent-being pulled off his head and Merelda let out a scream, but it turned out to be a young man wearing a mask. "He's fake like this tree," Merelda whispered to calm herself.

There was a huge burst of applause from the audience. It grew louder and louder through the closed drapes. Merelda wondered what was happening out there, and she noticed that the people in the fancy costumes on stage looked confused, too. Then the audience's applause stopped abruptly as there was a scream followed by a crashing sound. Chairs scraped backwards, and an instrument fell to the ground with a loud twang. Through the curtain, Merelda heard a man's voice shout "We need a doctor!" and the sound of a woman sobbing, then hundreds of voices began speaking all at once.

Ella's Choice

The scene faded from view. With great effort, Merelda made her tense body relax. She was standing on the windowsill inside Ella's dismal living room as if she had never gone anywhere, and Ella was still sitting and staring at the broken trophy on the ground. Ella's Potent was no longer in sight.

Merelda realized that her goggles were in her hand now instead of on her face. She hesitated, not sure if she wanted to put them on. She was tired again and felt vaguely sick. Merelda sat down on the edge of the windowsill and began cleaning her goggles with the edge of her apron. When they were as clean as clean can be, she set them down carefully and reached into her yellow and pink polka-dotted pocket. Out came a vial with a cork pushed firmly into its top. It held a special reviving drink with minerals in it that Tater and Tot had made for her, and she had charged it in the sunshine so that a bit of Father Sun lived in it, too. She drank some of the clear liquid, then poured a little into her hands and splashed it on her face. She set the vial next to her for confidence and put on her special goggles again, spinning the dial settings on the sides of the eyepieces three times a bit harder than she needed to.

Ella's Potent was sitting beside her on the windowsill, which gave Merelda a start. She hadn't realized the Potents could become as small as her current size, or that they would ever come so close to her while she couldn't see them. She was tired of being startled, so she grunted "humph" in her best impersonation of Tot, but she immediately felt guilty about it. She reached down and offered her drink to the Potent, but the beautiful Spirit-being shook her head and began talking.

"You asked what made Ella the way she is now. I took you to see the day in Ella's past when everything changed for her."

Merelda wanted to say that she would appreciate a warning before being whisked anywhere, but she bit her tongue instead and waited for the Potent to continue. A spider was weaving her web in one corner, and Merelda watched her as she listened.

"Just as the curtains were closing, Ella stepped through. She began

dancing again for the audience, performing a quick but difficult routine she had created and had never shown anyone. It was the most impulsive thing she has ever done."

Merelda fidgeted and felt agitated. So Ella had wanted to show off. Being the star of the show hadn't been enough for her.

The Potent continued. "Ella had never practiced the routine in that setting, and certainly she'd never practiced with a bouquet in one hand. The stage was crowded with the curtain behind her and the edge of the stage in front of her. But once she started, she felt she had to finish. She fell off the stage and into the orchestra pit, and the fall broke her hip."

Oh. Merelda looked over to where Ella sat looking grey, and she felt sorry for her. She didn't wish Ella's experience on anyone. The worst part was that Ella had brought it completely on herself. "Does her hip still hurt?"

"Her bones have been healed for a long time now. Ella could dance again, if she wanted." They sat in silence for a while, the only sound the shifting of a log on the fire. Merelda glanced at it and saw that it had almost gone out.

"What can we do for her, Potent?" It was an important question, and Merelda had chosen her words carefully. Merelda wanted to hold her wand in her hand, but she did not reach for it.

The Potent remained quiet. When she spoke, it did not seem in response to Merelda's question. "Ella has chosen to be as you see her right now. She could have learned from the accident, traced it back and looked into what motivated her impulse to get in front of that curtain. She could have gained great insight into her need for approval."

The Potent sighed and stretched her arms before her, a

graceful gesture. *"After her hip healed, I hoped she would dance again for herself rather than for others. There were other things she was good at, too, that could have taken her life in a whole new direction. I was ready to guide her into a future rich with new experiences."* She sighed and placed her hands calmly into her lap. *"But Ella has learned nothing from her fall except how to sit within a bubble of despair. She does not respond when I work with her, and at this point, I am not to become involved unless she asks for my help."*

Merelda couldn't sit still any longer. She felt a burst of energy to do something, anything. She was NOT like Ella.

House Cleaning

Merelda grew larger as she flew to the center of Ella's living room and drew her wand. It was clear that Ella's trophies and other ballet memorabilia held the bulk of the despair in the room. *"I could take that shelf down right now,"* Merelda said. It was a statement, but she meant it as a question. She turned to the Potent, her brows and her wand raised.

"It would be better if Ella took the items down herself," the Potent said. But there was a twinkle in her eyes that had not been there a moment before.

Merelda briefly entertained the idea of casting a spell directly on Ella, but she quickly dropped that line of thinking. Instead, she flew over above Ella's head and gazed out at the room, trying to see things from Ella's perspective. The fireplace with its depressing mantle was right in front of her, but so was the big window. The drapes looked heavy and oppressive. They reminded her of the theatre curtains Ella had impulsively stepped through that had led to her fall.

"Those curtains are a terrible addition to this room," Merelda pointed out. The Potent nodded, so Merelda raised her wand and sang out:

> "Curtains heavy upon the rod
> To me you look dense, unforgiving, and odd.
> Become thinner a bit each day, if you would
> And let some light in, the way curtains should."

Merelda held an image in her mind as she said the spell so the curtains would know what to move toward. The spell took, for the curtains immediately looked less heavy. "That was a good step," Merelda said, both to herself and to the curtains. Farmer Tom's home and her garden were in the direction the window was facing... A thought began to present itself, but a small sound broke her concentration and made her glance down. Ella's head was now sagging forward, and she had clearly fallen asleep.

"How about a bit of vacuuming?" Merelda asked the Potent.

The Spirit-being smiled. "I vacuum every night. Throughout the day Ella releases more despair, and it fills everything again. But yes, let's work together on that." The Potent hopped down from the windowsill, becoming human-sized as she fell so that her legs hit the ground impossibly quickly and her head shot up and blocked most of the drapes from view. Merelda stared. Is this what it was like for the creatures that watched her change size? Perhaps she should avoid letting others see her change in the future.

The Potent stretched her arms out to her sides, grew several more feet in height till her head nearly brushed the ceiling, and started humming. Black sticky worm-like tendrils began emerging from the walls and all the objects in the room and sucked into the Potent's open palms, where they vanished. The pungent smell of rotten fish filled the air with each new wave of black ick, but thankfully the smell faded almost immediately after the ick was absorbed. Globs reminiscent of huge black slugs came off the sleeping Ella, as well. They landed with an audible *splat* over the Potent's heart region, but they sucked into her and disappeared, as well. The Potent looked relaxed, like this was normal.

Merelda was mesmerized. She worked with plants this way, but their troubles were much more like watered down syrup. She wondered if she could handle this sticky-looking stuff...? Her curiosity got the better of her.

She held her wand out like a music conductor and sang:

"Wand, become like anteater
And suck up all that is ill.
But please do not keep it,
Put it instead into the dill."

Over the years, Merelda had learned that her dill plants knew how to convert other plant's ills into nutrients that made them thrive. Visitors always complimented Farmer Tom on his outstanding pickles, and Merelda often giggled as she overheard him trying to explain why his dill had such a strong flavor. She hoped this human variety wouldn't overwhelm her tender plants, and vowed to go check on them tomorrow morning to see how they were doing.

Several black tendrils attached themselves to the tip of Merelda's wand, and she was relieved to see them enter and have their horrid smell disappear completely. She decided to concentrate on the detail-work, as the Potent seemed to be handling what came of its own accord quite well. She flew up onto the mantle and gingerly tucked her wand into the corner-places on the trophies, encouraging the trapped wisps to enter her wand.

They worked this way together for many hours, Merelda poking and prodding in her most thorough way while the Potent walked through the rooms of the house, humming. Merelda tried humming the Potent's tune as she worked, and discovered it helped the icky substances go down more smoothly. Only twice did she have to stop the wand to remove a clog; all other times, they moved through on their own after she gave the wand a good shake.

Finally, the job felt complete. And thankfully, her wand seemed no worse for the experience. *"We're a good team, Merelda. This is the cleanest the house has been since we moved here,"* the Potent said.

Merelda blushed and curtsied in response. *"Goodnight, Potent. I'm sure I'll see you again soon,"* Merelda called from the windowsill.

She stowed her wand, shook out her apron, and took off her goggles. She was about to slip behind the curtain and out the window when she stopped. What would be the harm? She took one side of the less-heavy curtain in her hands and flew it to the near-by tieback attached to the wall. She tucked the fabric so Father Sun's light would be able to enter the living room. After checking to make sure Ella was still fast asleep, Merelda flew back into the room to inspect her work from Ella's perspective. "Yes, Brother Wind could have done that," she mumbled to herself. Just visible through the window was a large Black Walnut tree.

Merelda tapped her lips, considering, then gave her head a shake. "Enough is enough for one night," she scolded herself aloud. She flitted out the window and into the yard.

She gave the area a quick look and decided there was nothing here that loved each other well enough for her to hang her purple pocket. "We'll have to do something about that..."

Merelda flew home to her garden in the full dark. She hung her purple pocket in one of her customary spots on a strong energy line between a lettuce and a radish plant. Just before she entered, she sniffed the air to see what the chances were that Sister Rain would visit overnight. She had no desire to find her purple pocket plastered to the side of Farmer Tom's rain boot again, thank you very much! The chances were slim to none for a visit, but since the plants liked Sister Rain so much, she made up her mind to send an invitation her way soon.

"Goodnight, beloveds," Merelda sang out to her garden as she pulled back her purple fabric. Then she was inside her tulip-home and asleep quicker than a worm wiggles.

CHAPTER 5

The View from Ella's Window

The next day after all her chores were done and she had chatted with the dill (They were thrilled with the new variety of ick!), Merelda flew back to Neighbor Ella's house. She didn't go into the house, but settled instead just outside the window she had used last night. There was a planter box under the window that had seen better days, and Merelda used her foot to scuff some of the worst dirt away before sitting on its edge.

The curtains behind her, she was pleased to see, looked a bit thinner, but not so thin as to be obviously enchanted. They were still opened enough that some light and breeze entered Ella's house. No sounds came from the interior of the home.

An idea had started coming to her last night, but she had been too tired after all that vacuuming to pursue it. It had something to do with popping a bubble...

Merelda sat and gazed at the view Ella would have from her window once her curtains grew sufficiently see-through. There was a flat, mostly grassless lawn bordered by a series of overgrown hedges and one huge and oppressive looking Black Walnut tree. "That tree is taking most of Father Sun's light so it never reaches this house," Merelda murmured.

A walnut pod detached itself from the canopy of the Black Walnut tree and *thunked* to the ground, leaving an indentation on the earth. The green pod broke open upon impact, and brown juices oozed out onto the ground. Merelda got the strangest feeling that she had just received a warning, but she shook it off. Most trees were nice creatures.

"I'm sure you'd be a joy to know," Merelda whispered to

the Black Walnut tree. Another walnut pod launched itself toward the earth, and Merelda cringed. She found herself thinking of Billie B's sheriff's badge… She didn't like to think of what kind of rules this tree was enforcing.

She got on her feet. She had a hunch about what must be done next, but she didn't like it one bit. She pointed her wand skyward and called out:

"Father Sun,
Shine down for me.
Reveal what my next steps
Are supposed to be."

Father Sun heard, and answered. A strong beam of light shone down. It fully illuminated the Black Walnut tree. One smaller ray of light squeezed past its leaves and landed on a patch of ground much closer to her, just outside of the area that was littered with fallen walnut pods. Then the light faded as though Father Sun had gone behind a cloud.

Merelda took to the air and flew to where the smaller light beam had touched the bare earth. She became her biggest size, then dug there till she had a nice-sized hole. She surrendered to intuition, and her hand reached into the turquoise and yellow striped pocket that had held the sunflower seeds a few weeks back. Surely they were all gone? No, there was a rather large one hidden deep in the fold of the pocket. Merelda held it before her eyes and looked at it. "Would you like to sprout here?" Merelda asked the seed. She listened closely, and heard a *"yes"* that was louder than most seeds could manage. "Now that's interesting," Merelda mused.

She pulled out her wand and cast a spell that was a variation of the vacuuming spell she had used last night.

> *"Wand, become like elephant*
> *And spew out all that I need.*
> *Help me grow this sunflower;*
> *It is ready to be more than a seed."*

Damp, rich earth flowed from the tip of her wand till the hole was filled. She gave her wand a shake to turn it off and rubbed the tip against her darkest apron pocket so the dirt wouldn't show. Merelda whispered a fairy blessing into the seed, and a black stripe appeared upon it in answer. She smiled and tucked the seed into the new earth. She decided to visit it every day to help it grow up big and strong. When it did open its bloom to Father Sun, the sunflower would face away from the house. Ella, if she gazed out her window, would be looking at the back of the sunflower's head. "Who are you for, little seed?" Merelda asked. But now that it was in the earth, the seed couldn't answer.

Merelda glanced back at the house and the empty window. All was quiet. Then she gazed around the yard once more, stalling before her next task. Something near the base of the walnut tree caught her eye. It was one of the wandering mushroom babies! Merelda became a daintier size and flew over to scoop it up.

"What are you doing so far from our garden?" Merelda asked with a laugh as she lifted the mushroom and held it firmly. The mushroom nodded its head to and fro in answer, and light shone out through the white dots on its red cap. Adorable, Merelda thought, and she said aloud, "Your light is welcome here." Then a harsh *wock-a-wock* sound made her look up. Myrtle Magpie had just landed in the Black Walnut tree.

Myrtle Guards Tree's Door

Myrtle jumped to the ground next to Merelda. Startled, Merelda changed her size so that she was much larger than the bird. If Myrtle noticed, she didn't react. "*Wock-a-wock.* Merelda, I found you! I love my fairy gift!" She bumped into Merelda in her enthusiasm. Turning her body so the mushroom baby was protected, Merelda took several steps away from the magpie. Myrtle took this as an invitation and hopped closer.

"That's great, Myrtle. The color suits you." Merelda tried to make her voice sound cheerful rather than annoyed. The new purple feathers that covered Myrtle's chest were remarkably vibrant. Myrtle was a Yellow-Billed Magpie, and even before the fairy gift, she had been a beautiful bird. There was no other bird in the world that looked like Myrtle now. She noted with approval that Myrtle's white tummy was free from signs that she had ever been poked by the sheriff's badge.

"*Wock!* I repay you. I guard so no one steals purple pocket." Myrtle said this loudly and with such conviction that Merelda flinched.

"That's not necessary."

A walnut pod thudded to the ground near them. Both fairy and bird jumped back. Myrtle threw open her wings and jumped in front on Merelda. "*Wock!* You need protecting!"

"No, I don't. I was about to go inside this tree. Nothing will harm me there." It was the truth, or so Merelda hoped. She had been about to see if the tree would let her enter.

"I go with!" Myrtle squawked.

Merelda was exasperated and becoming quite cross. "No, Myrtle, don't come with me. I'm fine."

"I guard." Myrtle spun on one foot to face away from Merelda and stood up as straight as she could. As she spun, her extra long tail feathers knocked Merelda's feet from under her. Merelda landed on her bottom and shot Myrtle a dirty look before she remembered her manners. Thankfully, no one but the mushroom baby saw her do it, and he merely shined brighter in response; mushrooms like dirty things.

Merelda pulled out her wand to make sure it was still in one piece. It was. If Myrtle wanted to stand guard, fine, but she had business to do.

Merelda turned to face the dark brown bark and deep fissures that covered the trunk of the Black Walnut tree. She had been a friend to many trees in a surface, acquaintance sort of way. She lounged on their branches and sometimes hung her purple pocket between two acorns that were in love. On occasion, the Tree Spirits would talk to her, but for a real conversation she knew you had to go inside the tree.

She had only ever entered one other tree—a Jacaranda tree. Once a year, when Merelda's wooden wand began to run low on magic, she would take it back to its birth mother. The tree always opened joyfully at her wand's touch, and the journey within was a pleasant and rather thrilling experience. After the elegant Tree Spirit renewed the wand, Merelda would do some housekeeping, mending energy rips here and there, as a way to express her gratitude for being permitted within the tree.

She suspected this Black Walnut's Tree Spirit would not be as gracious. Regardless, she had asked Father Sun for guidance, and now she had to act.

She took to the air, flying slowly up the trunk and looking for a likely notch. She found one a third of the way up the trunk of the tree. The brown bark around the notch gave off a strange spicy smell. Merelda placed her wand's tip against the notch and hesitated for a few moments before she asked, "May I come in and talk with you, please?"

The notch opened with a rumbling sound, and within a few seconds a large round hole gaped before her. Merelda sneezed as she got hit in the face with a cloud of strong smelling tree-dust. She heard Myrtle flying up behind her, so she became small and darted a short distance into the hole in order to not be bumped by the magpie. She was grateful to have the mushroom light in her hand, as the passageway that led deeper into the tree was dark.

"*Wock!* What this?" Myrtle landed at the edge of the new opening and peered inside.

"It's a door. If you ever find a hole on a tree, then some fairy forgot to close the door behind her when she left, or she's still in there," Merelda said rather stiffly; she prided herself on being a tidy fairy. "I'm going in. You stand guard, okay?" Merelda was surprised to discover that she was actually glad Myrtle was there.

Myrtle spun around quickly, but this time Merelda was able to avoid being knocked over. As she put away her wand and began walking down the rough wood tunnel, the spicy smell was all around her. It reminded Merelda of the time Farmer Tom had roasted chili peppers and everyone had to leave the kitchen for a while until the scent had faded. Merelda reached her hand up and pinched her nose closed so she wouldn't sneeze again. "The Tree Spirit will be friendly, you'll see," she whispered to the mushroom baby, but she was really speaking to herself.

Into The Black Walnut Tree

The circular passageway curved to the right, and Merelda
soon realized she was walking in a spiral. It had to be a spiral, because
the curve was slowly getting tighter
and tighter. She held up the
mushroom baby as she walked,
and although her arm was
growing tired, she was still quite
thankful for the light.

She suspected she was nearing the center of the tree, for the tight inward curving was making her dizzy and the pungent smell was getting stronger. She stopped, wanting her head to clear before she went any farther.

"Why are you taking so long?" shouted an angry voice.

Merelda felt something jerk her by the front of her apron and lift her into the air. She swiftly shot around the last several turns. When she reached the center of the spiral, she was abruptly pulled face-first down a hole in the center of the tree. The sensation of falling was terrible. She struggled to right herself, but whatever invisible thing had latched on to her still had her in its grip. She screamed.

She was abruptly released. It took all her powers of flight to land on the fast-approaching ground with her feet first and slow enough that she didn't hurt herself. She saw in a blink that she was in some sort of earthy wooden chamber. She was furious. She had never been treated so rudely in all her life!

"You don't like being summoned?" The voice came from somewhere out of sight. "Would you like me to suck you into a wand-tip to be digested by dill plants?" Before Merelda had a chance to respond, she was jerked forward again. In front of Merelda was a huge circular opening in the wood that had NOT been there a moment before. Could this actually be a large wand-tip? The opening was trying to suck her inwards. She resisted it with all her might and hovered mid-air at the entryway. Her clothing and hair and even the tips of her wings were being pulled into the opening; she could not see in any direction but forward.

The voice came again from behind her. "What if I decide you're too thick, like the curtains? Would you like to be made thinner?" There was a crunching sound as the owner of the voice moved closer behind her. Merelda felt herself change. She looked at her outstretched arms. They were becoming see-through.

"Stop this at once!" Merelda shouted. There was an instant change. Where there had just been the opening before her, there was now smooth wood. Merelda flew backwards mid-air, crunched painfully into the owner of the voice, and fell to the ground. The spicy smell filled her nose, and she sneezed.

"Watch where you're going, stupid fairy."

Merelda looked down at her arms—they were solid again, and thankfully the mushroom baby looked unhurt. She scrambled to her feet and moved away from the voice, then turned to confront it. Before her was the Tree Spirit of the Black Walnut tree. His face looked like an opened walnut shell, with big strange eyes where the meat of the nut would have been. There was nothing else to him; he appeared to be just a head floating in mid-air. It exhaled a gust of the spicy smell.

Merelda stared at him for several hour-long seconds. She was trembling all over, but when she spoke, her voice shook only slightly. "May I speak without you attacking me?"

As her words reached him, his body appeared, but was gone again quickly. Merelda thought it had looked like it was filled with interconnected roots and armor made of bark, but she couldn't be sure.

"Oh, was I having no regard for you? Like YOU have no regard

for the things you interact with?" The Tree Spirit sneered at her. "You want me to fall so your new human project can get more light, don't you? If you could just knock me over, you would. You're the one that attacks."

Merelda was so startled that she felt her mouth drop open. Then the Tree Spirit suddenly let out a cry and jumped backwards. His body appeared again, and a gnarled, root-like hand pointed at her and shook. "Ah! You've brought a *fungus* into me! That's how you plan on killing me!"

"Oh, no, this mushroom baby is here for light."

A wand suddenly appeared in the Tree Spirit's hand, and brown tree sap shot out of the tip of the wand and engulfed the mushroom baby. It dripped down onto her left hand and abruptly hardened. Merelda was left with a big see-through chunk of amber encasing her hand and the mushroom baby. It had all happened so quickly that she hadn't had time to move or even think.

Tears came into Merelda's eyes. This was all *so mean*. She held her encased hand up so she could see the baby. A dim light was faintly visible around the cap, so it was probably still alive. Her hand felt heavy, and she felt sad and weak at the knees. A very old but familiar feeling of hopelessness welled up within her and lodged in her throat. The feeling triggered action, for whenever Merelda felt this way she always turned to the same place. "Take me to see Father Sun," she said quietly.

The Tree Spirit froze. "Father Sun? He's not your father; you can't call him that. You're just a stupid fairy!" Her words affected him strangely, though. He began crying. Great globs of spicy brown sap squeezed out of his odd eyes. They dried as they fell and made a clicking sound when they hit the floor.

Then he disappeared and reappeared beside her. His smell was so overwhelming that Merelda's eyes stung. She wanted to recoil from him, but he clamped one root-filled arm around her so she was pinned against his side. He raised the hand with the wand and Merelda experienced the same nauseating jerk she had felt before, only this time it jerked them both upward. Within moments the cavern was gone and all she could see was the small wooden tunnel they were now rising through. They flew upward at an alarming speed.

The Treetop Transformation

Merelda shot upward through the center of the Black Walnut tree with the Tree Spirit. She tried to change her size to get out of his grip, but his magic seemed to prevent it. They suddenly careened to the left, then right, then left again, and she couldn't think what to do but hold on. Her teeth rattled at the abrupt changes of directions, and the walls of the tunnels were growing closer and closer till her body was bumping painfully against them. When she tried to kick her legs to get away, she skinned her shin and scraped a knee against rough wood. It had been growing darker, but now the tunnel narrowed so quickly that it became impossible to see anything. They were going to slam into a wall! Merelda screamed, and they came to a sudden halt.

The Tree Spirit loosened his grip on her. The tunnel was so tight that even though she wanted to move away from him, she could not. He nudged the tip of his wand into a tiny notch and a fairy-sized opening appeared. Light streamed in, and Merelda felt a fluttering of hope. She tried to become her smallest size, and found now she could. She wriggled her way out through the hole and away from the wooden creature as fast as she could.

As Merelda crawled out, she relished the taste of fresh air. She carefully pulled herself to her feet and blinked around. She was standing on a small twig at the very top of the Black Walnut tree. Then she heard a noise and spun around. The Tree Spirit was squeezing out of the opening, all limbs and root-windings and horrid head, and she backed away from him as far as she dared. The twig shook from their combined weight, and its dozen long pointed green leaves rustled.

A light suddenly shined on Merelda so strongly that her eyes snapped shut. She was bathed in sunlight. *"You have been extremely brave, Daughter. Thank you for bringing the Tree Spirit to me."* The voice and heat were Father Sun. He was here! Merelda felt the light move so that it was coming from beside her instead of in front of her. A warm, firm hand was placed on her shoulder. She risked peeking out through squinted eyes. Everything was so intensely bright that she could see nothing of Father Sun, but she could just make out the form of the Tree Spirit facing them a short distance away.

Father Sun spoke to the Tree Spirit. *"Son, you were charged with the task of growing this tree. You have done a fine job. This tree has used my light to grow tall, and its leaves have breathed freely with this world. Soon the tree will fall and its wood will be used for many things. This is as it should be. For your work, I thank you."*

There was a long pause, then the Tree Spirit nodded. Merelda could not interpret the expression on that strange face.

"But you have much to learn about fairies. You misjudge them. So you will stay my Son here for a time longer, but you will now become a fairy and learn about their role firsthand." The light became blinding again.

When Merelda hazarded a peek, she saw a fairy boy standing before her where the Tree Spirit had been. Instead of having a face that was a walnut shell, there was one on his head as a hat. He had brown hair and green eyes, and was dressed in a simple tan shirt and pants with a leaf-belt. He looked terrified. Merelda noticed that he still held the wand in his hand.

"Your name is Aramon."

Aramon backed away from Merelda and Father Sun. Brother Wind began to blow, and all of the leaves of the treetop moved accordingly. Aramon surprised Merelda by leaping to a nearby twig. He ripped a leaf off the twig, held it over his head as though it were a parachute, and jumped from the top of the tree.

"Let him go, Daughter." Merelda hadn't realized it till Father Sun spoke, but she was hovering mid-air and had been about to dash after Aramon. It was to make sure he was okay, right? Merelda felt suddenly confused about how she felt about this boy. Did she want him to be safe?

Tears came into Merelda's eyes. She asked Father Sun the important question. "Should I believe any of the things he said about me?"

Father Sun grew large around her till she felt she was leaning back against him, and then somehow it seemed she was sitting in his lap. She closed her eyes against the blinding light and let herself be rocked. *"Let the hurt go."* As best she could, Merelda relaxed and did as she was told.

A vision appeared in her mind. She saw hundreds of tiny white threadlike objects attached to her body but stretching away from her, floating in the breeze. Most were coming from her head, but many were attached to other parts of her body, as well. The white threads were akin to individual spider web strands, and many of them had a small white cocoon trapped somewhere along their length. She heard a humming sound, and Father Sun's hands began gently pulling back the folds of thread that made the nearest cocoon. A tiny blob of black gooey anger had been trapped within; it absorbed into Father Sun's hand. He stroked the white threads till they became smooth and straight, then moved on to tease apart the next cocoon.

Merelda had no idea how long they sat together like this. The gestures and humming were hypnotic. At some point, Merelda realized all the cocoons were gone, and every strand glowed with light. It was beautiful.

The vision faded. Merelda sat quietly for a while longer, savoring the warmth of Father Sun. When she opened her eyes, the

sky began turning pink all around her. "Was I once a Tree Spirit like Aramon?" She had to know.

"You were once a Tree Spirit, yes. This is why you work with a wand, and that is why Aramon had to do what you said." Merelda tensed at these words. "Did you not notice? Your words had power over him. He brought you to me because you told him to do so."

"But no, you were not a Tree Spirit like Aramon. You were like you. I made you a fairy under different circumstances, and for different reasons."

Merelda wondered if it was polite to ask more questions. She was about to when she noticed that the sky was very pink now. "I am setting, Daughter," Father Sun said as he helped her stand.

"Thank you," Merelda said. Father Sun made the words echo off each leaf of the treetop as he assumed his place in the sky. It was a symphony of gratitude, and Merelda's place was in the center of it.

CHAPTER 6

Waking Myrtle

As the sound faded, Merelda turned and looked all around her. She realized with a start that the mushroom baby was gone from her hand. Where was he? Had he been placed in a pocket? She patted around gently and found that he was wrapped in a shiny new golden cloth and nestled inside her green lace pocket, fast asleep. All traces of the tree sap were gone from them both.

With a deep sigh, Merelda began flying home. She wanted to be in her own realm deep inside her purple pocket, wrapped in her lilac-petal quilt. Something niggled at her, however. Had she mislaid something? She patted around her many pockets and verified that her important items were in their places. No, that wasn't it. Oh! Merelda tut'ed at her own bad manners, spun promptly around, and flew back to the Black Walnut tree.

Merelda found Myrtle asleep. Myrtle had rested her head on her back and nuzzled her bright yellow beak under her feathers.

The position looked most uncomfortable to Merelda, and that horrid spicy smell was still wafting out of the tree's opening. Merelda was eager to close the tree-door and be away from this place.

"Thank you for keeping guard," Merelda said politely. Myrtle didn't react. "Time to wake up," Merelda said in a much louder voice. Still, there was no response. Merelda tapped her lips. It wouldn't do to leave with Myrtle thinking she was still on guard, not that she looked very much like a guard right now. "Attention!" Merelda shouted and snapped her fairy fingers. "You are DISMISSED!"

Myrtle stirred slightly, then opened one eye to regard Merelda. She gazed at her for a time sleepily. As she began to close her eye again, Merelda felt exasperated. She drew her crooked wand and called out:

"Myrtle Magpie, you must wake.
Do it now, for goodness sake!
Leave at once this wicked old tree.
Fly out this door and toward me."

Myrtle woke with a start and flew right into Merelda. *"Wock-a-wock!"* she screeched as her wings batted Merelda from left to right. Merelda had no choice but to throw her arms around Myrtle's neck and hang on tight. Myrtle was in a complete panic; she flew straight forward as though something was chasing them. "Wicked old tree! Wicked old tree!" she shrieked. Merelda craned her neck to see where they were going. Just as she got her head turned round, she saw Myrtle fly through the opening of Ella's window and straight into the fabric of the drapes!

Merelda clung to Myrtle's neck as they slid down the fabric to land with a bump on the ground. Then Merelda jumped up and got as far away from the panicked bird as she could.

She heard footsteps and looked up to see Ella staring down at Myrtle, her eyes wide with shock. She was still wearing the fluffy blue bathrobe, and she was holding a large pot covered with soapsuds. "You're the Yellow-Billed Magpie I saw earlier!" Ella said. She sounded excited. Then Ella did the strangest thing; she dumped the soapy water in the pot out the window, gave it a quick drying with her robe, and plopped it upside down over the surprised body of Myrtle Magpie.

The Joy-light Feeding

"What AM I doing?" Ella said as she stepped back and wrung her hands. Myrtle could be heard *wocking* under the pot, and the pot gave a little jump as Myrtle smacked her head against it. Ella's eyes were lively with excitement as she grabbed the marble base of the broken trophy and put it on top of the pot.

"Yellow-beak can't stay there for long. Where will I put him?" Ella began looking everywhere around her room and pulled several objects from cupboards in the kitchen, but nothing seemed to be what she was looking for. Finally Ella dashed over to her big glass-door china cabinet and regarded it with her head cocked. "You'll have to do!" She threw up her hands and began emptying the cabinet's contents. There were more ballet items and trophies here. Ella pulled them out and piled them in front of the fireplace next to the broken trophy.

While she worked, Ella kept up a happy stream of babble, with several refrains of the Mother Goose rhyme "Sing a Song of Sixpence" mixed in. "Not that I'm going to put you in a pie! Oh no, that's just a song. And you're not just any black bird; you're one of the rare Yellow-Billed Magpies!" All the activity caused Ella's brown hair to burst loose from her bun; it came down in bunches that cascaded down mostly the left side of her head. On the right side the hair-band was still stuck to one chunk, creating a strange sideways pigtail effect.

Merelda hid nearby beside the drapes and watched Ella's progress. She felt very jumbled up inside. She wanted to enjoy Ella's happiness, but she was too upset. There were long moments when Ella wasn't looking at the pot, and Merelda found herself mumbling, "I must free Myrtle!" and "How am I going to lift the pot?" Merelda fished a shoehorn out of her orange cotton pocket and was about to enlarge it when she heard a voice.

"*Let's just see what happens, Merelda,*" came the whispery high-language of the Potent. Ella's Potent! Merelda found her goggles where they lived atop her head and swiftly pulled them down.

After three adjustments to their settings, the Potent came into view. She looked as happy as happy can be as she worked with Ella. Through Merelda's goggles, she saw that golden joy-light was bubbling up out of Ella's heart region. It came in small bursts, as though a valve there was being turned for the first time in a long time. The Potent helped the golden light emerge from Ella, and she sent puffs of it out into the room so the items in the room could suck it in and store it. The scene was the opposite of the vacuuming session! The golden

light gave off a smell that was a mix of sunshine and baking bread.

"They were hungry. It's been so long since they were given anything they liked." The Potent's eyes were dancing with delight.

Merelda was torn. She wanted to be delighted, too, but… *"Potent, it's my fault this bird is trapped. I fuddled her mind with a spell. I have to set things right."*

The Potent looked like a seamstress working with a person that would not hold still. She sighed happily as Ella dashed over to add a pair of well-worn pink ballet slippers to the pile in front of the fireplace, then began tugging at the light that was emerging from her heart-region again as soon as Ella came near her again. *"Merelda, why aren't things right? Sometimes what we view as a blunder can be used to accomplish great things."*

Merelda was annoyed. She didn't want to talk to the Potent; she wanted to free Myrtle! Ella had already removed one interior glass shelf and was now laying paper along the bottom of the china cabinet. Soon Ella would finish preparing the china cabinet and would move Myrtle. *"Potent, I see how this is good for Ella. I do NOT see how it is good for my bird-friend."* Was the Potent stalling till it was too late? Did she only care about Ella?

The Potent's response was simple. *"Nothing is ever just for one person; if others are involved, there is something there for them, too."*

The Potent paused as she sent a stream of Ella's light toward the very pot that held Myrtle. The pot absorbed it happily. *"Myrtle is a magpie. Has she ever stolen something and kept it against its will? Today, she has the opportunity to be held against her will. She could learn a great deal from this experience, or she could learn nothing. Is it truly a mistake that she is here?"* Now the Potent did turn and look directly at Merelda.

Merelda's cheeks flushed a bright red. The desire to dash out and free Myrtle had been so strong. When she thought of doing it now, it made her feel selfish. *"Thank you for talking with me, Potent."* Merelda looked down at her feet. *"Perhaps I was fuddled, as well…"* All of a sudden Merelda had a thought that surprised her. *"Hey, did you just cast a spell on me?"*

The Potent laughed out loud at this. *"Well, not on purpose. But words are powerful; they can create change."*

Merelda thought about this as she put the shoehorn away in its orange pocket. She had never considered that her mistakes could actually help instead of hurt. *"I'll still try not to make mistakes,"* Merelda muttered. She felt a bit lame as she said it, though.

The Potent smiled. *"I have a favor to ask of you. Tonight, when Ella falls asleep, she will have an important question to answer in her dream. Will you stay and bear witness?"*

Merelda nodded. Then she realized the Potent was tugging on Ella's heart energy again and was not looking her way, so she spoke aloud. *"Yes, I will."*

It seemed they were done talking, so Merelda took off her goggles to give her eyes a rest. It was going to be a long night.

Something New

Ella placed one last object into the china cabinet, then turned and came to where Myrtle was trapped. She was holding a large piece of cardboard in her hand. "This won't hurt at all, Yellow-beak, but mind your feet." Ella shimmied the cardboard under the pot so that Myrtle was trapped between the pot and the cardboard, then she carried it all over and put it inside the china cabinet. Ella secured a green wadded-up washcloth into the door opening so that even when the china cabinet's door was closed, there would be a sizeable crack to let fresh air in. "I could get in through that crack," Merelda mused. Then Ella used a piece of wire to wrap the two doorknobs of the cabinet together so Myrtle couldn't push the door open.

When she finished, Ella stood on her tiptoes in excitement. "Shall I get that heavy pot off you? I want to see you, Yellow-beak!" Ella slipped the long handle of a ladle in through the door opening and jimmied it under the handle of the pot. With a swift motion, she flipped the pot so Myrtle was released into the display case.

What a squawking was heard! Myrtle screeched as she darted around the enclosure and smacked into the clear glass windows several times. Merelda couldn't watch—it was too upsetting. But eventually, Myrtle settled down and began exploring the objects Ella had put in the enclosure for her. When Merelda finally risked looking her way again, Myrtle was pecking at a sparkly purple gemstone earring.

The drapes Merelda hid behind were mostly transparent now, but Myrtle didn't look for her there. It was clear that Myrtle had forgotten how she had come to be in the house. Merelda felt guilty, but also made a point to keep her mouth closed. There would be plenty of time to apologize to Myrtle later, she assured herself.

Ella talked to Myrtle for some time, sharing with her as though she was a long lost friend. When she said, "I searched the Internet and there wasn't a single Yellow-Billed Magpie shown with a purple chest like yours; I bet a zoo would love to have you…" Merelda cringed and vowed to change Myrtle's feathers right that instant. She already had her wand out when Ella said "…but I'd never do that. You like living free and flying through the skies, don't you?" Perhaps Ella would release Myrtle after all.

Somewhere amongst all the talk, Ella retrieved a hairbrush and

tamed her wild hairdo. Merelda took note that Ella elected to keep it down rather than pulling it into a bun again; the choice was an improvement. It served to soften Ella's gaunt features, and all the activity brought color to Ella's pale cheeks, too.

She was changing before Merelda's eyes, but the biggest shift came when Ella produced a canvas and began painting a picture of Myrtle. Each brush stroke seemed to enliven Ella more and more till the space around Ella was humming with the magic of transformation.

With her brush, Ella captured large swatches of the shocking purple of Myrtle's chest and the vibrant yellow of her beak. The rest looked not one bit like a real bird to Merelda's eyes, and Ella was adding swirly details to the sides that made no sense to Merelda, but it didn't matter; the very air was vibrating with Ella's powerful act of creating something new.

Finally Ella yawned and settled down in the chair in front of the fireplace to go to sleep. Merelda thought Ella was about to drift off when her eyes snapped opened and she sat up. She walked to the mantle over the fireplace and methodically took down every item there. She added them to the pile in front of the fireplace and took off her customary blue bathrobe with its threadbare patches. She draped it over the lumpy ballet items so they were no longer in sight. Now that Ella was wearing a simple white nightgown, she looked surprisingly girlish. She placed her new painting on the mantle, then settled back into the chair under a plush blanket from her bedroom. Within a few minutes, Ella was asleep.

"Merelda, it's time. Put on your goggles." Merelda sat up and rubbed her eyes. She must have been about to doze off, too. She smudged her goggles as she pulled them down, so she had to clean them before putting them on. After three spins to their special dials, the Potent appeared before her, fairy-sized and very somber.

"Most nighttime dreams I give Ella when I'm vacuuming. Those are

designed to bring troubled emotions to the surface so I can pull them off her. But this dream will be different." The Potent's eyes began to glow with light, and Merelda's skin prickled. "Ella's decision tonight will affect her path through creation."

Merelda didn't understand what the Potent meant by this last statement, but she prickled all over with excitement and nervousness for Ella anyway. Perhaps she could help?

"The dream will be from Ella's point of view. No, you won't help; you will bear witness." The Potent placed one hand over her own eyes, then reached out and placed her other hand over Merelda's goggles. Merelda had just enough time to notice that the Potent had read her mind and that her goggles were going to be all smudged again before the room faded from view.

Ella's Dream

It was mid-day and Ella was outside. There was a huge concrete building in front of her. It had no windows, and the only way in was through the big closed double doors that were a short distance in front of her. There were no trees, no bushes, no grass—just the building with the doors.

Ella wanted to enter the building. She was barefoot and was wearing her simple white nightgown, but this didn't bother her in the least. It didn't bother her because right off she knew she was dreaming. She felt excited about entering the building, and in real life she never wanted to go anywhere or do anything, so this *must* be a dream. She began walking toward the big concrete doors. They looked extremely heavy, but there were door handles.

"Stop." The voice rang out from her left. Ella looked, and there was an Asian man standing there. "Only one of you may enter. The other has to go to the end of the line."

Ella was confused. There was only one of her. But then she realized someone was standing next to her on her right side. It was a thin, angry-looking woman wearing a ballerina costume.

Ella turned around to look behind her. There was a line of people stretching as far as her eye could see down a concrete road. The people were tiny in the distance and the line appeared to have no end. Everything about the scene was lifeless, including the people. Some held trophies in their hands and others wore fancy outfits, but they all had a bland look about them. The ones closest to Ella gazed at her with dull eyes.

Ella turned to face the Asian man. When she spoke, her own voice surprised her; it sounded clearer than Ella had ever heard herself sound before. "I would like to enter now. But if I am not allowed to, I will leave instead of going to the back of the line."

"Then enter," the man said with a bow. The woman to her right dissolved with a popping sound, and with a thrill of excitement Ella pushed open the doors and stepped within.

Ella looked around as the doors closed behind her. She was in a brightly lit place that seemed to be a mix between a luxurious shopping mall and a museum. No one was in sight, and she could vaguely tell there were walkways and displays. But the truly perplexing thing was that objects were shimmering everywhere at the threshold of being visible, but nothing actually *was* visible. Everything Ella considered had no form, but it sparkled with mystery and *almost* had form.

Ella was exhilarated. She began walking around and looking where she sensed there were objects. Shapes and sizes and colors flashed into her perception, but there was nothing she could latch onto and identify. She was in a giant display room filled with ideas she had never had and with thoughts that were entirely different than anything she had ever thought.

It felt wonderful to be here. The very air vibrated with creativity.

Ella stopped at one

display and considered it for a long time. The vague concept of "travel" came to mind. Something here took shape so that it was just barely visible. Was it a ticket, or a travel brochure? Ella felt she was just about to turn the corner on figuring it out when a flash of purple and yellow flapped by.

She instinctively turned toward it. "Yellow-beak!" Ella called out joyously. The Yellow-Billed Magpie landed not far from her on what might be a table. It gave her a purposeful look, then turned and flew deeper into the space towards a large staircase near the back of the room.

Ella followed the bird, and once she started, that was all she did for a long time. At first her pace was a walk, but before she had made the choice to do so her body was running as fast as it could towards the distant flutter of wings. Her barefoot feet smacked down on the marble floor, and the *smack smack* sound kept her company as she ran.

That smacking was so unlike how a ballerina *should* sound that Ella felt a thrill deep down of rebellion.

She ran up stairs and around corners, though passageways and sunlit rooms filled with more objects that were not quite there. Ella soon was very disoriented and knew she could never find the entrance again, but it didn't matter. The only thing that mattered was to keep the bird in sight and to move. It felt delicious to be moving! Somehow she never got tired, and that part of her that judged her and told her she was silly and useless and to just give up wasn't telling her anything. Not one thing! It was a blessed relief. She giggled aloud and pirouetted, then continued her pursuit. Always, the colorful bird was visible in the distance, till he was not.

Ella slowed herself from a run to a walk. Where had the bird gone? She found she was in a long hallway that ended with another pair of double doors. She *smack smacked* to the doors. When she reached them, Ella was shocked to discover that her painting of

Yellow-beak covered every inch of the doors. Here were the wild splashes of bright purple and yellow, and there along the periphery were her swirly patterns. They looked like an ancient language to her now, and some of them even glowed with light. A large one that throbbed gently began to swirl across the painting until it surrounded the door latches. Ella took this as an invitation, and pushed open the doors.

❧ ✄ ☙

A beautiful woman sat in a chair in the center of the room. Her body gave off a faint light, and Ella felt a thrill of recognition at the sight of her. She beckoned Ella forward with graceful fingers, pointing to a nearby chair. A wave of calm washed over Ella as she sat down and faced the lady.

The mysterious woman looked at Ella kindly with a smile that traveled well into her eyes. *"Do you truly want to do this?"* she asked in a high-pitched, whispery voice. Ella felt a mild confusion. What is she talking about? But something in Ella understood and began responding to the question. Ella felt like she was filling up and expanding several feet in all directions, becoming bigger than she normally was. The space around her became very dense. She noticed that her hands were radiating heat although they were lying still in her lap. Ella made herself take a deep breath and asked, "Do I truly want to do what, exactly?"

"To begin to fulfill your potential." The words came to Ella from a great distance, as though they were traveling through a tunnel. "Yes," Ella heard herself reply immediately. The sound

115

of her own voice startled her, as Ella hadn't chosen to speak. With the question, it was like when Ella's knee had been hit in the doctor's office; some unknown part of her had kicked in response.

The air around Ella pulsed. She blinked, and the room went gray for a moment. Although she hadn't moved, the woman in front of Ella was now hard to see. She swam in and out of focus, as though various lenses were being placed before Ella's eyes. But Ella knew somehow that what was important was to keep gazing into the lady's eyes. Fear and questions built up within her, but that steady gaze kept them at bay. Those eyes were a lifeline.

"*No matter how hard it is?*" the woman asked.

"*Yes, of course,*" Ella said, and she meant it. There is a steely calm resolve to her answer that again surprised her.

"*Then let's begin. Your part will be to let go of the old and let the new into your life. Trust and listen for guidance. We will do this together. The process won't be easy, but if you stick with it, you will make great progress. We would have you know fulfillment.*"

The woman nodded to Ella and stood up. Ella blinked, and for a moment, the woman looked like everything Ella had ever wanted to be. She *was* Ella.

The room dissolved.

☙ ℬ ❧

Merelda was again standing near the drapes, which she noticed were fully transparent now. The Potent was standing next to her. Merelda's goggles were too smudged to see through properly where the Potent's hand had touched the lenses, but she didn't mind. She was trembling from the experience of Ella's dream. Merelda took off her goggles and watched Ella slowly come awake in the chair in front of the fireplace.

Ella stretched and sat quietly for some time. When she got up, she walked over to the door of the house and wedged it open. Then she walked over to the china cabinet and unwrapped the wire that held its doors closed.

"Thank you for taking me where I needed to go, Yellow-beak. I hope I get to see you again." Myrtle let out a faint *"wock"* before she took the sparkly purple earring in her beak and flew out of the house.

Then Ella sank to the ground, and cried and cried till there was finally room in her for something other than tears.

The tree fell the next day.

CHAPTER 7

Farmer Tom's Bubble

When the children got home from school, they didn't want to do homework. They wanted to play! Lila Ticklegums was the first to emerge from her father's car. She shouted over her shoulder, "Last one to the lemon tree has to drink warm whale pee!"

Giggling madly, she ran pell-mell toward the lemon tree that grew on the far side of the house. As she rounded the corner, she heard her brother's footsteps right behind her and feared she might lose. But all thoughts of the race went out of her mind as she skidded to a stop.

"Whoa…" Lila breathed.

Billie B stopped running, too. "Papa!" he called out. He felt scared. He dashed back to the car and grabbed his father's hand. "Come," he said, tugging hard.

"Hang on a minute. We've got a visitor." There was a black pickup truck parked in their driveway. Leaned back in the front seat, seemingly fast asleep, was Cowboy Roy. Farmer Tom grinned at his sleeping friend and let Billie pull him in the direction of the lemon tree.

When he rounded the corner of the house he froze, then gave a low whistle. The garden stretched out before him, terraced so that it rose along the gentle slope. Normally, a huge Black Walnut Tree stood at the top of the slope just beyond Farmer Tom's land. The tree had fallen.

Its trunk was now angled down the slope and its leafy canopy stopped just shy of the children's play structure. Neighbor Ella's yard and house, usually screened from view, was clearly visible. Farmer Tom squatted next to Billie and put his arm around his son's small shoulders. "What do you think, Billie?"

"I don't like it," Billie said. "Put it back the way it was."

Farmer Tom watched as his daughter Lila climbed the slope and began inspecting the fallen tree up close. He gave Billie a squeeze. "I know how you feel."

There was the sound of a car door, and soon Cowboy Roy joined them. "Well I'll be," he mused. After a long pause he added, "You sure had it nice before, huh? There goes your bubble."

Farmer Tom looked at his friend and felt annoyed. His bubble? Cowboy Roy had that slightly superior look on his face that was infuriating. Farmer Tom didn't feel like figuring out his statements. But then he did figure it out, and sighed.

"Oh, yes. Well, I wouldn't have put it that way, but yeah, I see what you mean. No more privacy..." Farmer Tom sighed and ran his fingers through his bushy brown hair, causing a few patches to stand up even more straight than usual. "A lady lives up there by the name of Ms. Ella Becken." He glanced down to make sure he was wearing closed-toed shoes; his hairy feet were nobody's business but his own. "Guess I best go talk to her. Want to come?"

Cowboy Roy raised an eyebrow and nodded. They began up the path.

When they were near the top, Lila hopped down from where she had been walking along the trunk of the fallen tree. She grabbed her father by the arm. "Look, Papa. I didn't want to go to Neighbor Ella's house ever again, not ever, but then I saw that." She pointed.

Facing them from the center of Neighbor Ella's yard was a single brilliantly yellow sunflower.

The Snake's Slither and Other Ministrations

It had been a busy day for Merelda.

Merelda had just finished her morning rounds of blessing each plant in the garden when she heard a tremendous crash. The Black Walnut tree had fallen! After she got over her initial shock, the rounds had started again. This time Merelda used her wand to suck up the blackish fear from the stalks of the plants before replacing it with extra blessings.

Then when she went to the tunnels that ran under the garden to return the mushroom baby to Tater and Tot, she let herself get talked into helping them put each plant's roots in a pot. "They'll be needing extra minerals to calm themselves," Tot had explained, "and we could use a hand getting their roots in the pots."

"This is gnome's work," Merelda grumbled to herself as she stirred some amethyst powder into a pot full of muddy water and tried to coax a nearby broccoli-root to have a sip. The gnome's tunnels were spacious enough, but Merelda did NOT like being underground. It was dirty, and all those roots poking down from the ceiling of the tunnel didn't look orderly to her eyes.

"Try it, you'll like it," she said to the broccoli-root in an annoyed but motherly tone as she held out the pot, but the root kept trying to investigate her pockets instead. Merelda had to pretend to drink some herself before the stubborn root would let herself be dipped in. As she turned to consider the next plant in the row, the broccoli-root prodded her quite roughly in the back to ask for more. "You unruly root!" Merelda scolded, but after a quick glance down

the tunnel to make sure Tater wasn't looking her way, she put another pinch of amethyst powder into the pot.

Merelda was pleased when a messenger worm's rounded face poked through the wall of a tunnel and called out, "Gimble Gopher's stuck in his hole." Merelda excused herself from the gnomes' mineral ministrations and found her way back to the surface as quickly as she could. She wanted a bath, but Gimble would have to come first.

Gimble Gopher's most recent batch of home-holes were located at the top of the garden and they were now under the fallen tree. When Merelda arrived to the area, she found that Gimble wasn't stuck, but he was scared. Merelda landed on a branch near a hole and tried to convince him to make the trek across the garden to his other set of holes down by the oak tree, or his set of holes by the lemon tree, or the really big set in the front yard. Gimble poked his head out to talk to her, but he would duck back into his hole again mid-sentence. "How can I..." he started, "...know that another..." Merelda sighed and practiced her patience. "...tree won't fall on me?" Gimble was panting from his efforts of going in and out of his hole.

"I'll walk with you, Gimble. It'll be okay." Merelda was wondering how long this was going to take when she heard a nearby hissing noise. "Wait here, I'll be right back."

Merelda flew this way and that, trying to locate the source of the hissing sound. When she found it, she tapped her lips. Now this WAS going to take a long time. Merelda didn't have to put on her special goggles to know what had happened. She flew down and patted the snake on his head. "Poor Silas, the fall must have really startled you. I'll just go tell Gimble what's happened, then I'll find and reattach your slither, okay?" The snake's tongue flicked out in answer. "You just wait right here," Merelda said, then felt foolish. Of course Silas would wait right there—he couldn't move without his slither!

Gimble wanted to wait, so Merelda donned her special goggles and located the energetic slither. It looked very much like a see-through snake except that it had no head or tail, and it had red energy grids where there would have been scales on a physical snake. Merelda bruised her elbow struggling to get the uncooperative slither back over to Silas, but she was trying not to think about that.

And so it was that Merelda found herself settled down near the roots of the fallen Black Walnut tree with a black and orange striped garter snake in her lap and an energetic slither partially pinned under her left leg.

"Silly Silas," Merelda said as she stitched. "You're going to lose your whole snake skin over this." Every time a snake's slither slips, the fairy's stitching makes the snake's skin shed. Silas was unable to do anything but hold perfectly still as Merelda used her magic needle and thread to reattach each scale to the corresponding energy grid on the bright red slither, but oh how that slither slipped and slid!

Merelda had to wear her special goggles to see the slither and she had to wear magic gloves to maintain a good grip on the

123

slither, too. The gloves made it especially hard to wield the needle with precision. But although her eyes and hands were busy, her ears were perfectly free. When Farmer Tom and his family came into Neighbor Ella's yard, she was able to hear their conversation from where she worked.

"Well, you best go ahead and knock," prompted Cowboy Roy.

There was the sound of knocking, then a door opening. Merelda hazarded a glance and saw that Ella looked softer than she had the day before. Although her eyes were puffy from last night's crying, they had lost their pinched look, and her hair was loose down her back. Where her simple floral dress hadn't protected her she had a sunburn, but that suited her, too. There were a dozen or so boxes labeled "donations" on her front porch.

After Cowboy Roy was introduced, Farmer Tom began to talk about the tree, but Ella didn't seem to be listening to him. She kept looking at Lila until Farmer Tom noticed and got quiet. "I was, umm, rude to Lila a few days ago," Ella explained. Then her voice dropped and she must have mumbled an apology, because the next thing Merelda heard was Lila saying brightly, "That's okay. My room shines with light for me." Merelda couldn't help but grin; oh, how she loved Lila Ticklegums!

   The children left the adults then and climbed up on top of the tree-trunk together. Thankfully, they weren't able to see Merelda and the garter snake unless they actually looked under the tree in exactly this spot. But the rattle of the tree was distracting and annoying, so Merelda began working as fast as she dared.

   "Black Walnut tree's wood can be used for flooring and tables and all kinds of things. This tree could bring you some money,"

Cowboy Roy said. Farmer Tom said he would contact his friend that worked at a local sawmill to find out if they would remove the tree. Although Ella said something about sharing any profit, Farmer Tom wouldn't hear it.

"No, no. No need for that. But hey, here's another good thing that will come out of all this. Now you'll be able to grow a garden, if you want one."

Farmer Tom began talking farmer-talk about how Black Walnut trees give off a toxin that poisons the soil so very few things will grow, and how you can't put even the leaves in your compost pile. Farmer Tom seemed to realize then that Ella didn't know what a compost pile was, so he launched into an explanation of the benefits of keeping your food scaps to give back to the land. After he ran out of facts to share there was a long pause, then Farmer Tom offered to help Ella start a garden in her yard.

Merelda could tell from the sound in Ella's voice that she was nervous.

"I would like that, although I'd have no idea where to start or how to keep it nice or anything." Here Ella's voice faltered. "Your garden, it's so... May I? I mean, is it all right if I don't put another tree here? I get a lovely view, but now you'll see me, and I'm, well..."

There was a long silence. Merelda stopped her stitching and looked up to see Farmer Tom's response.

"It's okay. And I'll help you get your yard in order, like I said. It'll just take time. You'll see." There was another long pause as Farmer Tom fidgeted and began pulling up the nearest batches of weeds. "And I'd be grateful to help, to tell you the truth. I need to take my mind off things at times, and gardens do wonders for that. My yard didn't always look like this, no. It was all weeds when we first moved in."

Then Farmer Tom's face turned beet red. "Listen, I'd... Well, I've already got one guest, so I was wondering if you would like to come, too." He gestured at Cowboy Roy, who was picking up walnut pods from the yard. "To dinner tonight, that is. The food won't be amazing or anything, but I do have really good pickles, and I'll come up with other things to offer, I always do. And it would be a real treat for us guys, and Lila, too, to have a lady around."

Ella blushed and accepted the invitation. The Potent words from last night came back to Merelda's mind: *"Nothing is ever just for one person."* When Merelda turned her attention back to her snake-stitching, she found that her hands were trembling.

Hot Lava

It was nearing dusk when Merelda watched Silas Snake slither away. A long transparent snakeskin lay on the ground as testament to her work, and Merelda moved it carefully out in to plain sight so Billie B could find it more easily. Then she went to see if Gimble Gopher still wanted to relocate to another set of holes. He did, so she waited patiently as he ducked in and out of his opening several times, then joined her for the walk across the yard. "I hha... hhhhate being out in the open," he said as his big yellow front teeth chattered in fright.

The children were visible in the distance jumping between several big piles of leaves near the pathway that led through the garden up to the house. Merelda knew they were playing a game called Hot Lava where you weren't supposed to touch your feet to the actual ground and had to stand instead on something. "Whose winning?" called Merelda as she and Gimble got close enough to be heard.

"Fire, Fire! The ground is made of lava!" shouted Lila Ticklegums. Merelda immediately took to the air with a chuckle, but Gimble began running in circles, not realizing this was a game of pretend.

"Your feet are burning!" Billie B hollered to the gopher from his pile of leaves, and poor Gimble looked even more puzzled, running to and fro on the dirt path, trying not to let his feet stay in any one place too long.

Lila took pity and called out, "Onto the leaves, Gimble—they're safe." Gimble noticed then that each child was standing in a big pile of leaves. He scurried atop the closest leaf he could find, panting. Then he carefully picked up each paw to inspect the pads of his feet. Merelda landed next to him.

"Bother this!" Gimble squeaked. He took off running as fast as his little legs would carry him to the oak tree and that set of home-holes. Merelda felt sorry for him as he disappeared into the biggest hole. The children's silly game was not a good match for Gimble's mood today.

As Merelda stood watching him, she experienced the strangest sensation. It felt as though the soles of her feet were indeed growing hot! Merelda kneeled down and touched Mother Earth. She was as hot to the touch as a mid-summer day.

Merelda was just wondering if Mother Earth had a fever when she saw a movement out of the corner of her eye. A boy fairy was ducking behind a branch of the Black Walnut tree. It was Aramon! Merelda felt a wave of anger as she pulled out her wand. Had he cast a

spell? If he had, she would be able to lift it.

"Lava fresh within this earth
You do not cause us any mirth.
Go back from whence you came today.
Don't come again; our play is just play."

The ground immediately grew cool to the touch, but Merelda felt herself growing hotter. Of all the irresponsible things to do! Aramon had conjured LAVA into the ground of the garden. It could have burned the children or hurt her plants!

She flew to the hole Gimble had entered. "Are you okay down there?" Merelda felt a stab of panic at the thought of Gimble emerging with smoking whiskers, but he called out in a gruff voice that he was fine. After turning down his invitation for tea, Merelda took several deep breaths. "Everyone is all right," she said to herself.

The sound of the children's laughter washed over her, and moments later she heard Farmer Tom call them in to help with dinner. She realized she could use a bit of dinner, too. Merelda cast one last glance in the direction of the fallen Black Walnut tree, then went to find a good place to hang her purple pocket. As she pulled out her magic clothespins, she found herself remembering Myrtle's offer to stand guard. She shook her head sharply to free it from such thoughts. It was time to eat huckleberries, not to fret.

Merelda's Potential

Later that night, Merelda lay on a tree branch near Farmer Tom's house and sleepily plopped the last berry into her mouth. She had taken a dip into the pool in her fairy realm and she felt refreshed. The night sky overhead was filled with stars, and the sounds of laughter coming from below made her heart feel full.

She glanced down again and smiled. Gathered around the fire were Farmer Tom, Cowboy Roy, and Neighbor Ella. A short distance away, Billie B and Lila Ticklegums were putting together a puzzle by moon light.

Merelda gazed up at the sky and let her thoughts wander. Ella had gotten to see her Potent last night in the form of a dream..."I wonder what my potential would look like..." Merelda murmured to the sky. She closed her eyes till they were barely open and squinted at the lights in the heavens.

On a whim, she pulled down her special goggles over her eyes.

The stars shined brighter through the lenses, but otherwise were the same. Merelda daydreamed that the stars were dripping down into her and filling her with starlight. What a delicious dessert that would be...

"Adjust your goggles dial settings forward seven times, Merelda," whispered a Potent in high-language. Merelda was startled, but she obliged, carefully counting each *click.* Through the goggles, Merelda saw the stars overhead begin to move and grow even brighter as she made her final *click.* Smaller ones branched off from the bigger ones and formed new patterns in the night sky. Merelda gasped as the stars clumped directly overhead and formed a stunning galaxy formation that extended in all directions.

"What is this?" Merelda whispered the question to the Potent, but she did not look away. She was trembling with excitement. An idea was hovering just beyond her grasp.

"It is your potential, Merelda. The lights represent the joy you make possible for those you interact with. It creates a ripple effect, see?" The Potent's voice was admiring.

Merelda couldn't hold still any longer. She had to move! *"Thank you, Potent!"* Merelda said, and she flew up into the sky, looking and marveling. "Oh, to be a fairy!" Merelda called out as she flew. "Oh, to be me!" She flew straight up into the light as high as she could. She wanted to be in the center of the stars, and wanted to hug them all. She was quivering with joy.

Then, by chance really, Merelda looked down.

Through the goggles, she saw down on the land the same type of galaxy formation, but the lights were coming from the plants, the crickets, the snakes, the birds, the people; everything she interacted with was glowing with light. They made the same pattern as was overhead, only it was not as bright or extensive… yet.

"I am being shown what I have accomplished so far," Merelda whispered. She was frozen mid-air, too startled to move. "I did this." Her voice sounded very quiet. She didn't know how to believe it, but she knew it was true. She looked up again, then back down.

Tears came to her eyes. It was glorious and overwhelming, and somehow it made her afraid, too. Then Sister Rain was beside her in the darkness, in that middle place between the lights overhead and the lights below. Mereleda pushed back her goggles and together their tears fell down on the land. What the tears meant, Merelda could not say. She just cried till she was done. When she looked around again, she discovered Sister Rain was gone.

Still hovering mid-air, Merelda patted around her pockets for a handkerchief. She pulled out the new golden cloth that Father Sun had wrapped around the mushroom baby and brought it close to wipe her eyes, then blinked and looked at it more closely. This cloth had a golden-red fairy hair hem like her purple pocket did! Fairy hair marked it as belonging to a fairy, and as being a doorway… And the hair used to hem the fabric was *her* hair. That meant…

Merelda held the top of the golden cloth in one hand and used her other hand to pull back a corner of the fabric so she could peek inside. Golden light streamed from behind the fabric as though Father Sun himself was just behind the doorway. And he was. He winked at Merelda. She smiled her broadest smile, and winked back.

Then Merelda Manypockets folded the golden fabric and put it carefully back in the green lace pocket of her apron. Her goggles secure atop her head, she flew as quickly as she could for home. It was time for bed.

THE END

Author ❧ *Jodi Ember Roney*

When she's not writing, Jodi can be found singing and dancing with her musical theatre troupe in San Diego. She also loves to host parties that involve silly hats, exploding pies, face paints, and all things ridiculous and unexpected. She has a degree in biochemistry and does graphic design for biotech companies in her free time. She lives in Escondido, CA with her husband, two sons, her animal counterpart (a thoroughly furry Bernese Mountain dog), and Merelda Manypockets.

Illustrator ❧ *Natalia Zanfardino*

Natalia pursues traditional and digital arts, mural painting and graphic design, and though her style has taken on many unique forms, she still gets her greatest inspiration by observing bizarre insects, creepy creatures of the deep blue sea, and the magical wonders of the microbial world. She currently incubates in her Los Angeles studio where she draws, dreams and plans on creating much larger community spaces for the arts to thrive locally and internationally.

Made in the USA
San Bernardino, CA
12 June 2017